LOVE ME DEAD

D1359765

LISA RENEE JONES

ISBN-13: 978-1091111493

BE THE FIRST TO KNOW!

THE BEST WAY TO BE INFORMED OF ALL UPCOMING BOOKS, SALES, GIVEAWAYS, TELEVISIONS NEWS (THERE'S SOME COMING SOON!), AND TO GET A FREE EBOOK, BE SURE YOU'RE SIGNED UP FOR MY NEWSLETTER LIST!

SIGN-UP HERE:
HTTP://LISARENEEJONES.COM/NEWSLETTER-SIGN-UP/

ANOTHER SUREFIRE WAY TO BE IN THE KNOW IS TO FOLLOW ME ON BOOKBUB:

FOLLOW ME HERE:
HTTP://BOOKBUB.COM/AUTHORS/LISA-RENEE-JONES

DEAR READERS

Thank you so much for picking up LOVE ME DEAD! Before you read on, I want to warn you that while this Lilah Love case will standalone over its own two-book duet, there is a rich history to Lilah's life you discover in the launch duet—MURDER NOTES and MURDER GIRL. You will enjoy the series in a more fulfilling way if you read that duet first, before moving onto the next case with LOVE ME DEAD.

However, I do give you a glossary for a lot of key players in Lilah's past. I've tried to make sure new readers won't be too in the dark. I'm also including a brief recap, to familiarize yourself with where we left Lilah. So without further ado, please keep reading for said recap. If you have not read MURDER NOTES and MURDER GIRL, and don't want those books spoiled please stop reading here, as I will be spoiling the outcome of that case...

Lilah Love is an FBI agent with a crass attitude, a wide array of uses for the word "fuck," a strong aversion to blood, and the ability to solve any crime that ends with a dead body. Any crime that is except the one that chased her away from the Hamptons years ago after being attacked. But she knows who the murderer is in that crime: it's her. She murdered her assailant and her heir-to-a-drug-cartel boyfriend, Kane Mendez buried the body. What she still didn't know was *why?* That is until bodies begin to surface with the same tattoo her attacker had, a call to her past that she just can't ignore and resulted in her fateful return to the Hamptons. To her family. To the past she ran from. And most importantly, her return to Kane Mendez.

She may have returned to the Hamptons, but Lilah is there only to solve the case, and be on the first plane back to LA as soon as possible. However, driving forces outside of her control have other plans. Lilah is greeted home to another dead body that fits the MO of the previous victims, and she's also met with a taunting letter from someone she names Junior. Said letter alluding to a third party knowing what happened *that night*. The night Lilah killed. The night that changed her and Kane irrevocably. Speaking of, it's not long before Kane himself is wrapped up in her case and trying his best to be wrapped up in *her* as well. But even he knows all too well there are no coincidences, and something far more sinister is going on with these murders that Lilah is working on.

Try as she might, there is no separating her past from these current murders. They're fully intertwined as Lilah soon finds out, and there's only so much she can keep from her boss, Director Murphy, as she gets closer to more answers. These murders eventually lead Lilah to the discovery of the Society, a deep state-like organization set on masterminding government dealings behind closed doors and out of the public eye to their own benefit. It turns out both Murphy and Kane were aware of the Society long before Lilah was, and more shockingly, her father, former police chief, and now mayor of the Hamptons, is very much a part of the Society. And at the orchestration of Ted Pocher, one of the local leaders of the Society, Lilah's father will be running for governor of New York to further implant the Society in the government. All of this information in regards to the Society, comes with the most horrifying revelation, that they were responsible for Lilah's attack, and even her father knew about it. His only reply being when she confronts him with the ugly truth of her rape at the hands of the Society, is that she should be thankful they didn't murder her. It's clear as day, the life Lilah left here, is not the same one she's returned to. The only true constant is Kane, but even with him, she can't just fall back into the same routine so easily. He altered both of their lives the night he buried the body of the man she killed, and even though the attraction is still there, he's still the heir to his family's drug cartel, even though he's the CEO of a very high-profile and legitimate oil company as well. And Lilah's badge will always be between them when he's that close to the wrong side of the law. It was a problem back then, and it's a problem now. Only now, they also have to contend with Junior leaving more notes for Lilah in his taunting way, with Kane and Lilah no closer to figuring out his identity.

Thankfully, Lilah was having more luck on the other side of things with her murder cases, but it was turning more dangerous the further she dug. Yes, the Society was responsible for the murders, and yes, the Society was responsible for her attack, but to what end? Her attack was simply because she was getting too close in a case she had been working. Having entered a tenuous house of cards, rather than having her eliminated, the Society had her raped to send her a message to back off. In much the same manner, only the endgame was death, the Society was sending a message to the victims in Lilah's case. The victims were in the midst of trying to form a coup and take control of the Society, but those in power never gave them a chance to get close. This information comes from the elusive assassin, Ghost. He was thought to be the hired hand behind these murders, but informs Lilah and Kane that the Society has several assassins on their payroll and another one with the codename: The Gamer has been behind these killings. And there's one more name on the list to be killed: Eddie Rivera. An old colleague of Lilah's, the second son her father never had, and the husband to Lilah's ex-best friend. As Lilah and Kane race to save Eddie, it's already too late. The Gamer has killed him, and coming up on the murder, Kane and Lilah scuffle almost to the death with him, but like most times with Lilah, the perpetrator is the one who ends up dead.

Having had quite enough of just about everything and everyone, Lilah chooses to throw her badge away after The Gamer is killed. Nothing about her past or present is what it seems, and the only true constant in her life, Kane, will always be kept at a distance because of said badge. But while Kane may think she's making an error in judgement, he's going to give her time to think through everything she's learned, and all the illusions that have been shattered. However, one person won't let Lilah have any time to digest her new findings and altered reality: Director Murphy. No,

3

he's there, shoving her badge back at her, and tilting her world further on its axis.

Alongside all of this drama, Lilah had also made connections between the Society and Hollywood. Hollywood, the industry in which her mother used to work. Her mother who died in a plane crash several years ago. Only Murphy informs Lilah that not only was *he* in a relationship with her mother when she died in that plane crash, he also thinks it was intentional and orchestrated by the Society. And the Society is officially ingrained in every aspect of Lilah's life, she has no choice but to take Murphy up on his demand that she stay in New York and join his new task force that will be at face value exactly what she has always done: catch killers. But they will also have a singularly unique, and under the radar goal of getting the dangerous people who are in power, out of power.

Upon acceptance of her placement on the new task force, she moves more permanently to an apartment in New York. When she arrives, Murphy has delivered a case file on The Gamer for her to look over, he may be dead but that case is far from over, and a cold case of a serial murderer who goes after call girls. When she steps out for pizza Ghost waylays her. Seemingly enamored by the fact that she was able to do what he was not, kill The Gamer. He says she intrigues him and he owes her one.

As she arrives back home she finds a note. A note from Junior: *M is for Miss me? I missed you. D is for Disappointed. He's not for you. This city is not for you. S is for sorry. You are going to be so so so so so so so sorry. W is for warning. Don't say I didn't warn you.* But before she can dig deeper Murphy calls. The locals needs her help. They have three dead women and an active serial killer. She reminds him that they have one of the best profilers in the world, her old mentor. Murphy replies with he knows, because that's who requested her presence on the case. And so Lilah gets ready to be faced with one of the only people in the world, other than Kane, that she can't hide from. Only this man has yet to see the monster Lilah fears lives inside her.

LOVE ME DEAD

And that's where we pick things back up...

INDEX

Lilah Love (28)—dark-brown hair, brown eyes, curvy figure. An FBI profiler working in Los Angeles, she grew up in the Hamptons. Her mother was a famous movie star who died tragically in a plane crash, which caused Lilah to leave law school prematurely and eventually pursue a career in law enforcement. Lilah's father is the mayor in East Hampton; her brother is the Hamptons' chief of police. She dated Kane Mendez against her father's wishes. She was brutally attacked one night, and Kane came to her rescue, somewhat, and what unfolded that night created a secret between the two they can never share with anyone else. This eventually causes Lilah to leave and take the job in LA, away from her family, Kane, and that secret.

Kane Mendez (32)—brown hair, dark-brown eyes, leanly muscled body. He's the CEO of Mendez Enterprises and thought to be the leader of the cartel that his father left behind when he was killed. But Kane claims his uncle runs the operations, while he runs the legitimate side of the business. Lilah's ex from before she left for LA. He found her the night of her attack and shares that secret with her.

Director Murphy (50s)—gray hair, perfectly groomed. Former military. Lilah's boss. The head of the LA branch of the FBI. Sent Lilah to the Hamptons to follow the assassin case.

Rich Moore—blond surfer-dude looks, blue eyes. Works with Lilah. He and Lilah were sleeping together until Rich wanted more and Lilah called it off.

Jeff "Tic Tac" Landers—Lilah's go-to tech guy at the FBI.

Grant Love (57)—blue eyes, graying hair. Lilah's father, the mayor, and retired police chief of East Hampton. A perfect politician. Charming. He's being groomed by Ted Pocher to run for New York governor.

Andrew Love (34)—blond hair, blue eyes. Lilah's brother and the East Hampton police chief. Andrew is protective and seems to be the perfect brother. The problem is that he's perfect at everything, including being as macho and as bossy as their father. There's more to Andrew than meets the eye.

Lucas Davenport—tall, looks like a preppy version of Tarzan. A very successful and good-looking investment banker, he has taken to hacking in his spare time. He is a cousin of sorts to Lilah and Andrew. His father was the stepbrother to Lilah's father. His father was also known to be with Lilah's mother, Laura, on the night they both disappeared in the plane crash. He flirts mercilessly with Lilah, seeing as they're not blood-related, but she always shoots him down.

Greg Harrison—Lilah's old partner from the New York Police Department. Currently in a lot of hot water with Internal Affairs over an incident that may or may not be of his own making. He was partnered with Nelson Moser prior to being put on leave by IA pending further investigation but has been working independent security with Moser in the meantime.

Nelson Moser—a lowlife police detective who offended Lilah on numerous occasions before she moved to Los Angeles. She is not very fond of him, and the rumor circulating about him is that he's a dirty cop.

Laura Love—Lilah's mother. Famous actress. Died four years ago in a horrific plane crash. She infamously portrayed Marilyn Monroe in an Oscar-winning performance. Much mystery still surrounds her death and will be a recurring issue throughout the series.

Ted Pocher—billionaire CEO of the world's fifth-largest privately held conglomerate, Pocher Industries. Has taken a liking to Lilah's father in hopes of furthering her father's political career. He tried to do business with Kane and Mendez Enterprises but was turned down because of his rep for shady business deals.

Beth Smith—blonde, tall, thin. The new medical examiner in Suffolk County. Lilah's friend from back in the day. Beth is working one of the assassin murder cases.

CHAPTER ONE

It's a fucking disaster, a downpour of epic proportions, the mother of all storms, that came out of nowhere. The kind of storm that demands you hunker down in the company of Cheetos, strawberries, coffee and/or booze. The latter choice, at least for me, depending on how irritated I am at the world at the time. The kind of storm that makes you want to do those things inside and by a fire. Not here, walking the Manhattan streets, with no umbrella, on my way to a crime scene. I pull the hood of my rain jacket lower, down to my brow and round the corner to find a carnival of uniforms, flashing lights, and an ambulance that will be the ride to the morgue. Rarely am I called in when the victim lives to talk about the crime. Dead bodies are my thing. They talk to me. I understand them. Those who are still living and breathing, not so much.

My cellphone rings, and I halt, digging it from my field bag that rests at my hip. Glancing at my caller ID, I find Kane's number, when he's supposed to be on a plane, jetting off on the kind of business we don't talk about but we pretend is something it's not. Kane and I are both masters of pretending to be something we're not. Me, an FBI agent who would never cross the line. Him, nothing more than the CEO of Mendez Enterprises, a company deeply rooted in oil, not the man who took over the Mendez cartel when his father died. He damn sure didn't take on the Society, the deep state that secretly runs our government as some might call them, and force their retreat, even if only for the moment, with nothing but oil money. I decline the call, shove my phone back in my bag and start walking again. I can't walk onto the crime scene feeling like I'm as transparent as Kane makes me feel, and I can't think about the war we've managed to enter with the Society, at least not with this particular crime scene to think about.

Nothing about me being called in on this case, a suspected serial killer's involvement or not, makes sense, not when that request, per Director Murphy, my pain in the ass judgmental boss, came from my old mentor, Roger Griffin. Roger's NYPD. I'm FBI. I've never known that power hungry, grumpy old man to ask for agency assistance. Hell, he doesn't ask for help at all, and he doesn't need it. He's so damn good at what he does that he can look into the eyes of a killer and see a killer when someone else might see Mary fucking Poppins. I don't know what he saw in me when he snapped me up so many years ago and started training me. I just know that I don't want to know what he'll see now.

Cutting across the street, I beeline toward the yellow tape establishing the police perimeter, flashing my FBI badge at an NYPD ran site, and I don't stop walking, my strides steady right up until the point that I'm standing outside the building that is the crime scene. Fortunately, there's a small overhang taking the beating of the storm for me now, so I yank my hood down while watching an officer and his muddy boots enter the building. I step in front of Carl, the beat cop who just let that happen, a cop I've known from years back when I worked at the local NYPD.

"Lilah fucking Love," he greets, because this is my home base, this is where I got my start before relocating to LA with the FBI. Everyone here knows that I like the word fuck. The word fuck fucks with people. If there was a book about my life, it would be called "Lilah Fucking Love Says *Fuck You*." And then all those delicate people who get their feelings hurt easily would go away, thank you, Jesus. Unfortunately for Carl, before we're through here, he's going to be one of the people I offend. "Heard you were in LA working for the FBI," he says.

"And yet, I'm standing right here in New York City, wearing an FBI badge."

"Are you here to work the case?" he asks.

"No, I'm here to bring you lunch." I reach in my field bag and hand him a package of cheese crackers that are about a year old. "I heard it had been a long night."

"Smartass," he grumbles, staring down at the crumbled mess in his hand. "I see your attitude hasn't changed."

"You mean the one I learned from all you old-timers who thought I was too young to profile?"

"You were a kid when you started out. You still are."

I don't bother to tell him that twenty-eight is not a kid, or that my brother is North Hamptons' police chief, a job he inherited from my father, who is now the mayor. I stopped justifying my skills versus my age a long damn time ago, but my silence doesn't matter. Carl is still talking.

"Take it from me," he adds. "Opt out of this one. It's the worst thing I've ever seen."

In other words, a little girl like me just can't play with the big boys. "It's not the worst thing I've ever seen."

"You haven't even been up there yet."

"Exactly," I say. "I *should,* in fact, be up there right now, but you know why I'm not?" I don't wait for a reply. "I'm not up there now because I'm standing here wondering what idiot thought this spot where we're standing isn't part of the crime scene? Which idiot is that, Carl?"

He blanched. "I—the detective in charge—"

"Before you finish your sentence, there's a person who lost their life tonight. If that was your mother, father, daughter, son, or wife would you want muddy boots stomping past this door?"

His jaw clenches. "I'll handle it."

"Get a tarp here ASAP and set it up as wide as possible. We need the teams to be able to cover up and clean up before and after they leave the building."

"Got it. Handling it."

"Is Roger here yet?"

"Roger Griffin?" he asks. "I haven't heard any mention to him showing up. I thought that's why they called you."

He's wrong. Roger doesn't give up a crime scene. "Who exactly is in charge of this scene?"

"Lori Williams."

"Wrong answer," I say. "I am." I open the bag I have hanging at my hip and pull out a pair of booties, stepping close to the door to slip them on my wet feet.

Another cop, a big burly guy with brown hair, tries to enter the building. "Hey!" I snap. "Don't even think about walking in that door without covering up."

He glares at me. "Who the hell are you?"

"The girl who will bitch slap you, and it only took one meeting, if you don't do what *the fuck* I told you." I shove my hand into a glove and then repeat.

"That's Lilah Love, Reggie," Carl chimes in. "She's FBI and a profiler here to help. She's also a bitch. I'd take her seriously if I were you."

I give Reggie a condescending smile. "Don't worry. I won't turn you in to your boss. I'm not that big of a bitch. I'll just tell the family of the victim that we're sorry that the evidence was destroyed, but Reggie hates covering up, and we don't like to make Reggie uncomfortable."

"Bitch," Reggie bites out.

"Now you get the idea," I say, pleased that he's not the slow learner I'd suspected. I eye Carl. "What floor?" I ask.

"Ten," Carl replies.

I shrug out of my raincoat and drop it next to Carl because, unlike the rest of these assholes, I don't plan on contaminating the evidence with a dripping wet jacket. I enter the building, stepping into a small foyer with mailboxes to the left. Taking nothing for granted, considering the fuck show this has proven to be, I scan the area, eyeing the ground, and even looking up toward the ceiling. I find nothing of interest, but I repeat my scan because what we miss the first time, we might not miss the second.

I start the walk up the narrow stairwell, which must be a bitch to travel after a big meal or a bunch of booze. For a big man, it would require skill to navigate quietly, a detail that I tuck in the back of my mind for later review. Even without overindulgence, for someone who doesn't run five miles a day, much of it in the Hamptons on the sandy beach, like myself, this walk would be tough. That says something about the person who maneuvered the steps and disappeared without notice. Unless they were noticed. Maybe they belong here. Maybe they visit regularly. Maybe they're a delivery person.

Apparently ten is the top level, and that was too simple a description for Carl. I pause at the top of the steps and canvas the roughly seven-by-four foyer, another tight spot, in this case, a tight spot that would be hard to escape for a woman being overpowered. There's nothing here that presents like obvious evidence, just a few bagged jumpsuits waiting to be used, which tells me the scene is bloody. That's one of my dirty secrets. Despite my comfort level with dead bodies, I don't like blood, at least not in excess. Blood is actually fine. A bucket of blood, not so much. Blood to the ankles, which I've experienced, definitely not. I freak the fuck out. It's a weakness that I don't share with anyone, and yet, today, I'm asked for, by name, and the scene is bloody. Some might call that a coincidence, but as Roger taught me years ago and has always proven true, there is no such thing as coincidence. The fucked up part of this equation is that Roger knows exactly how I feel about blood. He was with me the first time I freaked out, the only time anyone of professional consequence has ever seen me freak out. Okay my ex back in LA might have seen a little bitty incident, too, but that was literally ankle deep blood, and he wasn't a superior of professional consequence.

CHAPTER TWO

Setting aside my personal hate for blood and the fact that I now estimate the amount beyond that apartment door to be excessive, I have questions, starting with: where the hell is the person who's supposed to be making sure we wear those bagged jumpsuits laying on the ground? If they're counting on humans being smart, they're stupid, which proves my point: someone should be on guard in front of the door, managing the integrity of the crime scene.

Oh, wait. There is no integrity to this crime scene, which is so poorly managed that I wish I was a drinker. I'd drink myself into throwing up and then check into recovery, where I'd survive a few days before my irritation at the people who couldn't control their urges would then cause me to beat some asses. Which would be highly hypocritical of me since I have a few urges I can't seem to control either, like killing people and ending up naked with Kane fucking Mendez. A thought triggered by the ringing of my phone in my pocket that is most assuredly Kane fucking Mendez.

I ignore the call simply because I don't want to ignore the call. Fuck you, Kane Mendez, for making me want to talk to you. Just because you buried a body for me doesn't mean you get to control me.

I grab one of the suits and dump my field bag on the floor. Reggie appears at the top of the stairs, hovering there. I have a bad history with the name Reggie. The body Kane buried for me bore a tattoo done by a guy who worked for a tattoo parlor owned by another Reggie. Therefore, if your name is Reggie that immediately puts you on the wrong foot with me. I shove my arms into my suit. He's still watching me. "Are you role playing for some practice session at the police academy and pretending to be a Peeping Tom or is creepy just your thing?"

"You aren't the detective in charge," he snaps.

17

"Did you know," I begin, zipping up my orange suit and wondering why cleanliness means looking like an inmate in this city, "that I was the girl most likely to in high school?"

"Most likely to what?" he asks, taking my bait, his thin lips thinning even more when they're already pencil drawings on his face. "Get naked?"

"Kill someone," I say, grabbing my field bag and sliding it over my head and across my chest, so I don't have to try to hold onto the damn thing when my feet and stomach are swimming in blood. "You wouldn't be my first," I add. "Put on a pretty orange suit or don't come into the apartment." I offer him my back and reach for the door.

"You *aren't* the detective in charge," he bites out, repeating himself, his limited vocabulary rather irritating, as is his need to get the last word.

That said, I've found that men who need the last word with a woman typically have deep-rooted confidence issues, in essence, little man complex. And since Reggie isn't little anywhere that I can obviously identify, I can only assume his lips aren't the only things pencil thin. I feel sorry enough for him to let him think he's won: I give him the last word.

I open the door and inhale the scent of iron, that distinctive promise of blood, lots of blood, but I don't find it. The scent is there, but the room before me is a simple, clean living space with an untarnished, basic cream-colored couch, and two pastel blue side chairs. Of the not one, but four, jumpsuit-clad forensic specialists working the tiny space and beyond in an open concept dining room and kitchen, not one of them so much as looks up to greet me. That's okay. I don't need to be greeted. I'm here for the victim and no one else. This is a crime scene, and while this space might be missing the body that is here somewhere, it could hold clues. I stand there, taking in every detail, eyeing the painting of an ocean on the wall and nothing more. There are no photos of people. No trinkets. No memories. This person is as fucked up as me. That means he or she doesn't let people close.

"Ms. Love."

At the sound of my name, I turn to find a thin redhead, I'd place in her mid-forties, who isn't wearing a jumpsuit. "*Agent* Love," I correct. "And were you afraid the orange would clash with your hair or did you just not give a fuck that you might contaminate the crime scene by failing to wear one?"

"I'm not rolling around in the mess that's been made," she bites out. "Nor should you. You're supposed to profile the killer, not perform forensic analysis."

Obviously, this bitch is Detective Williams, the detective in charge, but she won't be for long. "Where's Roger?" I ask, still trying to solve the mystery of how I got here in the first place.

"Roger said you can handle this on your own. Was he wrong?"

She's baiting me, but I'm not one to be baited. Roger called me in, but he's not here. Any relief I feel at avoiding his all-knowing inspection fades quickly. "Where's the body?"

"Down the hall in the master bedroom."

I start to walk in that direction.

"You don't want to know who she is?" Williams calls out.

"She'll tell me herself," I reply.

"You might want a barf bag," she calls out, making herself all too easy to read. Detective Williams is a walking, talking power trip out to prove that she's better than me. Which is why I don't bother to reply, and why would I? She's not important. The woman who lost her life tonight is another story. She matters. The person who took her life also matters, right up until the moment that we make them pay.

Cutting down a narrow hallway, the walls along my path are barren and the iron scent of blood now permeates the air with a vicious punch. I could work myself up about the buckets of blood that could be waiting on me, but that's just not how I'm made. I need to be punched in the face with the crime scene. I need to take it all in, feel the shock and pain, and do it without any reserve. And so, I enter my Otherworld, my zone where nothing but the crime scene

19

exists, where Kane Mendez and my shitty father don't exist. Where assholes that fuck up crimes scenes don't exist. There is just me, and the victim who needs me to speak for them. I step to the doorway of the bedroom and let the scene take over, clicking through what I find in what has become an almost mechanical process for me.

There is, of course, a dead body, a naked woman lying in the center of the room on her back. That's expected. What's not expected is the fact that she's holding an open umbrella above her head. She's been dead long enough that rigor mortis has set in, and her fingers are frozen around the handle. There is also blood, but not in buckets. It's dispersed in splatter marks on the walls, the ceiling, all over the white, neatly placed bedspread, and virtually every other spot in the room.

There's also an unexpected but familiar woman kneeling by the body, smartly wearing an orange jumpsuit. "Beth," I say, drawing her attention.

Her gaze jerks to mine, going wide in surprise. "Lilah fucking Love," she says, using her gloved hand to pull down her paper mask.

"Why is a Long Island coroner at a Manhattan crime scene?"

"I go where they send me," she says. "But it doesn't seem like a coincidence that we're both here, now does it?"

Considering she just worked a case with me that directly linked to the Society, no, no it doesn't, but she doesn't need my agreement. Not to mention she looks unsettlingly like the victim. This entire crime scene is starting to feel like a puzzle, and we're not the ones controlling the pieces. I need to change that and quickly. I cross the room and kneel beside the body, across from Beth, then look up at the ceiling fan that is holding a Tupperware container with holes in it.

"My understanding," Beth says, "is that the fan was on when law enforcement arrived."

A rather brilliant contraption that took time and some level of engineering to execute. I frown and look at her and then the body, my brow furrowing at the untarnished face and body, no cuts, no wounds. "I know what you're thinking," Beth says, "and you're right."

My gaze lifts sharply to hers. "The blood isn't hers, is it?"

"No. The blood isn't hers."

CHAPTER THREE

"Just to be clear," I say, motioning to the room. "I'm standing in a room that looks like a scene from a B-rated flick that's one-part horror and one-part porno." I hold up a hand. "Not that I watch either of those things—but I've heard, and you're telling me that the added cherry on top is that, that blood doesn't belong to the victim?"

"That's the general gist of it all," Beth confirms.

"If this isn't her blood," I say, "then whose blood is it?"

Beth lifts her gloved fingers. "Exactly."

"Exactly? That's not an accurate response to my question."

"It was exactly the right answer because that's exactly the question. Whose blood is it? Or perhaps, the real question should be, where's the other body? Because no one survived losing this much blood. There has to be another body."

I grimace and say the most appropriate thing I can think to say in this moment, "Fuck."

"Pardon my French," Beth chimes in, "but yes, *fuck*."

I give her a deadpan stare. "Did you just say 'pardon my French?' How fucking old are you?"

She visibly cringes. "I spent the weekend with my parents. Sometimes I'm terrified that I could become my mother."

"You should be. I'm terrified for you." I eye the woman on the floor and I'm instantly checked out of the conversation with Beth. This woman, whoever she is, will never see her parents, siblings, friends, or anyone ever again. "Who is she?"

"Mia Moore," Beth says. "Twenty-eight. A retired, but successful model, who worked in fashion for a high-powered advertising agency."

"Mia Moore," I repeat, my gloved hand touching her hand where it's been posed to hold the umbrella. This is

23

about power, about domination. This was done by someone who never feels quite as good as everyone else. Someone who feels overlooked. "Cause of death?" I ask, eyeing Beth.

"To be determined."

Considering Beth's years of experience, that says all I need to know. The answer isn't obvious, but I trust her to figure it out. "Was she raped?"

Her lips thin. "All I can tell you right now is that there are no bindings and no obvious struggle."

Which could mean she knew the killer or that she was too afraid to fight, which might mean a weapon was involved or threats to her family. "What do we know about her personal life?"

"I don't ask those questions. I want to go into the initial screening as blind as possible. I prefer to not even know what I already know in this case."

I give her a quick nod. "Understood." I scan the room and visually confirm what she just told me: there was no struggle. Everything is in order, nothing appears out of place. "Did she die here?" I ask.

"Based on the lividity of the body, yes, but I'll confirm once I do the official exam."

"I'll attend the autopsy." I try to head off any questions she might have about why we're both here, questions better discussed elsewhere. "That will be a good time for the two of us to talk."

"Right," she says, but for a smart person, she chooses to ignore my obvious avoidance. She lowers her voice. "Why are we both here, Lilah? It feels off. What is this?"

"A black fucking hole," I say, "where we bleed out if we're not careful." Because it's true. This, us here, together, is a warning, and I've made enough powerful enemies recently to take it seriously. "Which is why we'll act normal and talk later."

"Sometimes I really could do without your honesty," Beth snaps, pulling her mask back into place. Whatever. She can be pissy as long as she keeps her mouth shut, so I can, in turn, keep her alive.

I stand up and start a deeper inspection of a room that's really quite cold in its basic, sterile nature. Even the damn Kleenex box on the single nightstand sits in a perfect line. A white wooden dresser calls to me, and I pull out a drawer and then another. One after another, I scan and find perfectly stacked and folded items to such an extreme that I decide Mia had some level of OCD, which may or may not come from some kind of abuse in her youth. Abuse leads to an abuser. Some might think the blood means the killer doesn't have OCD, but I don't. The blood is part of a perfectly painted canvas. I just don't understand its perfection.

Yet.

I pull out my trusty camera from my bag, the one I use on the clusterfuck crime scenes like this one; aside from preserving the evidence these idiots might destroy, shooting pictures keeps me from shooting said idiots. And while the latter would be far more satisfying, as is the case with eating a half gallon of ice cream, indulging the inner demon that says "do it" has consequences. Which takes me back to pictures. My brow furrows, my mind trying to grab onto something I can't quite reach. My mind flashes back to one of the first cases that I'd worked with Roger. We were in Brooklyn, and the murder scene was painted black. Roger had known the paint hid a secret. He'd known there was a message somewhere in that paint, and he'd been right.

I glance down at my camera. It's creating a story I can visually read later, the way our killer created a story in this room for me to read right now. What if the blood splatter isn't a mess to sensationalize the crime scene? What if it's a well-crafted story?

Shoving the drawer shut, I lift the camera and shoot a good fifty shots of the walls, circling and shooting, circling and shooting. "Are you done in here?"

At the sound of Detective Williams' voice, my gaze jerks to the doorway where she stands, still too damn prissy to put on a jumpsuit. "I need to bring in the team to bag the evidence," she adds.

"They can wait," I say, as my attention lands on the wall in front of me, and I notice what I should have noticed before now. The splatter pattern stops in a perfect line a few inches from the corner. That line isn't an accident. I look up and then down, where I spy something lodged between the carpet and the wall.

"Agent Love," the bitch in charge snaps, but I ignore her. I do that with bitches. It works for me.

I close the space between me and that wall and kneel, trading my camera for a pair of tweezers and a baggie. Leaning in, I inspect the item I've discovered and pluck a used cigarette stuffed in the hole where the wall doesn't quite meet the carpet. A Marlboro. The same kind my mentor smokes. There are no coincidences. This is not an accident. This is a message. This is a warning.

CHAPTER FOUR

I want to stand up, drop the cigarette, and grind it under my foot, a little fuck you for whoever left it for me. Of course, I won't do that, not at a crime scene, but a girl can fantasize. Instead, I'll wait this out and stick the cigarette up whoever's ass is trying to mess with me right now. Considering the Society just staged a series of murders to cover up their wrong doings, and I just vowed to stay out of their shit in exchange for my life, this is starting to look dirty. This is starting to look like them daring me to come at them again, like them telling me they will hurt people I know—Roger, Beth, who knows who else—if I don't look away from this. Well, fuck them. I'm not looking away from shit.

"What the hell is it?"

At Detective Williams' demand, I bag the cigarette and stand up. She's hovering in the doorway as if she can't enter the bedroom in her street clothes, as if this is the only part of the apartment that's a crime scene. The entire building is a fucking crime scene in my book, but apparently my standards are too high for this woman. "*Agent Love,*" she bites out.

I close the space between me and her, simply because getting closer to Detective Williams is the only way to get the hell away from her. Or punch her. Showing rare restraint, I stop in front of her, rather than barrel over her, a strong hint for her to move, when I don't give a lot of hints, before I push past her. She doesn't move, but considering the really nasty vein bubbling up in her forehead that might be smart. It would suck to have to save her life while fantasizing about killing her. "What is it?" she demands, when I know she saw me studying the damn cigarette.

"A message," I say, shoving the bag at her, forcing her to grab it. "To me," I add. "It's a message that was meant for me, which is why I'm here."

"What?" She frowns, her forehead crinkling with deep lines as she does. "What message?" she demands. "In the cigarette?"

She's genuinely confused. I believe she spends a lot of time genuinely confused, but in this case, it helps me rule her out as a part of the Society. She's just too damn stupid to be one of those assholes. "I told you," I say. "The message is for me. Now step aside."

"Agent Love," she snaps. "This crime scene is mine and—"

"It is yours," I say. "Which is a good reason for me to leave."

Her lips purse. "I need a profile. If this murder is personal to you in some way—"

"They're all personal to me. Get me the data collected from the crime scene. Then we'll talk about a profile."

"You don't even know her name."

"Mia Moore. Twenty-eight. A former model turned advertising executive. I need the files on the other two victims as well." I reach in my bag and hand her my business card. "Email me all the relevant facts and details."

"There are no other victims."

What the fuck is this woman talking about? "I was told there was a serial killer and that there were three victims."

"Obviously, you weren't listening well," she bites out.

More like she doesn't know what the fuck is going on. My boss doesn't make mistakes. Roger doesn't make mistakes. They both said there were three dead women. That means there are three dead women. The question is, why doesn't the detective in charge know? Oh right. She's stupid. "Get me everything you have on Mia Moore," I say, done with her for now and always, if I get my way, and I'm going to get my way.

She snatches the card. "Obviously you're going to read the same crime data I will and tell me what I already know."

"I'm wearing an orange jumpsuit, and you aren't. I'm Frosted Flakes. You're Fiber Bran. I'm tequila. You're Kool-Aid. We didn't see this crime scene the same way from inception. We'll never see anything the same."

"Jesus help me," she growls, but she doesn't move.

"A religious person, are you?"

"Yes," she says. "I am. Is that a problem for you, Agent Love?"

"Do you know that story about the man who stayed in his house despite a vicious flood because he knew Jesus would protect him?"

"No, I don't." She folds her arms in front of her. "And please don't tell me."

"Well, the flood came, and it was bad. A fireman stopped by to help. The man turned him away. Jesus would save him. Later, a boat came by, and the man onboard offered to help. Again, this man turned down the help. Jesus would save him. The water swallowed his house, and he was on the roof about to drown. He looked skyward and asked, 'Jesus—why didn't you save me?' Jesus answered him. You know what he said? He said, 'Holy Mother of mine. I sent you a fireman and a boat. You ignored the help.' The man drowned." I narrow my eyes on her. "Do you know the moral of this story?"

"No, but I'm sure you're going to tell me."

"Yes. *I am.* This is Jesus helping you right now. Move or be moved."

She glares at me, but thank fuck, she backs up and allows me to pass. And so, I do—quickly. I head down the hallway toward the only door in this place. "Was that long ass story necessary?" she calls after me.

It kept you from talking, which kept me out of jail, I think, so yes, yes it was. I step into the living room, and the forensic team is gone. Of course, they are. Why would anyone do the right thing for Mia Moore? Clearly, she was on the bad side of the Society. I exit to the hallway, and there's still no one guarding the door. I strip out my orange gear and then head down the stairs, right as a familiar cop in uniform is headed up my way.

"Lilah fucking Love," he greets.

"Nick fucking on my nerves," I say, because yes, he's tall, dark, inked, and good looking, but he also hits on anything that moves, including me. "Got a wife and kids now?" I ask, passing him by without stopping.

"Not yet," he calls after me, and I can feel the way he's turned to watch me as he adds, "Want to try out for the job?"

I pause at the bottom of the steps and give him a once over. "Nope. Still not my type. I don't like guys who like themselves as much as you do. They're assholes. You're an asshole, but you're a good cop. Or you were when I left. Why aren't you a detective yet?" A perfectly self-serving question. I'm in town now. I'd rather deal with common sense. The last I remember, Nick qualified, and Detective Williams certainly doesn't.

"I failed the test."

"Try keeping it in your pants the night before. That was a serious remark. Get focused on the right things."

"Why don't you study with me? Come on over and get me focused."

I sigh at his incessant flirting. "Whatever. You could matter. Obviously, you don't want to."

"You think I don't matter now?" His tone is sharp, a whip that was a feather.

"I think you're below your pay grade. As far as I'm concerned, you're holding a spot some new fresh talent should hold." I turn to exit.

"Do you have an umbrella? You'll need it. It's still raining cats and dogs out there."

I freeze and whirl on him. "Do I have a fucking umbrella? Are you serious right now?"

"Yeah, Murder Girl," he says, using a nickname that started in LA when my team got creeped out by how comfortable I am with the dead; a name I didn't think he'd know. "It's supposed to rain for like two weeks solid," he says. "Some kind of monsoon overflow."

I stare at him, and suddenly, I don't like what I see in this man. He's in his late thirties, a player, who couldn't pass the detective test. He's smart enough. He just doesn't want to pass. Why? What's he hiding from? He winks, a fucking wink that makes me want to poke his damn eye out before he turns and starts walking up the stairs. It hits me then that he didn't even ask me why I'm here. He didn't act surprised that I'm here at all. I've lived in California for years. There's no way Nick thought my presence was to be expected. He wanted my attention. He has it. I am, after all, looking for a location to shove that cigarette left for me upstairs.

CHAPTER FIVE

I step outside to a downpour, rivers of water running along the curbs, a shower for a dirty city, and a disaster for a sensitive crime scene. "How bad was it?" Carl asks, still holding his spot by the door.

"Lots of blood and assholes, Carl," I say, eyeing an item on the ground by the door that I'd missed earlier, of course, so did everyone else. And why wouldn't they? To this crew, this isn't part of the crime scene. I reach in my field bag and snag a small baggie. Sticking my hand inside it, I squat down and pick up another damn cigarette, this one unused, and flip the bag the opposite direction to secure it.

"Whatcha got there?" Carl asks.

Pushing to my feet, I close the small space between me and him, shoving the baggie at him, the way I had the one earlier with Detective Williams. "Log it into evidence."

"That's probably from the crew."

"It's not," I say, and I don't explain my reasoning, nor do I bother to lecture him on proper crime scene procedures this go around. No one seems to care, and if I wallow in their crap much longer, I'll be the one with a vein bursting in my head.

Carl looks like he wants to fight me on this, but his lips press together, and he gives a nod. "I'll log it." I keep looking at him, and he adds, "Right away."

That's what I was looking for. I don't wait for him to do what he's agreed to do. Carl's reliable. He follows orders. His pal Reggie is a different story, and for all of Reggie's attitude, he has just disappeared. Another curious thing among too many tonight.

I grab my rain jacket that's still by the door, slip it on, pull my hood back up, and eye the twenty-four hour diner across the street and to the right. It's a perfect spot for a killer to have coffee and watch the mess unfolding near the crime scene. Works for me. The downpour does not. I eye an open umbrella next to the wall, grab it, and start a jog across the closed off street. Once I'm under an overhang in front of the diner, I drop the umbrella. Whoever it belongs to can come and get it.

Pulling open the door, bells chime, and I scan the rows of red booths. I'm the only person here. I'm the only killer here. It's a little disappointing. "Sit anywhere!" A plump black woman from behind the counter shouts at me.

I choose a seat by a window that allows me to see the fuck-up of a mess across the street, and shrug out of my dripping rain jacket. Once "Donna," per her name tag, joins me at the table, I ask for strawberry pie. "We've got pumpkin and pecan."

"It's October," I remind her.

"Fall flavors," she replies.

"I don't do fall flavors," I say. "I'll take coffee."

"Pumpkin, hazelnut, or plain?"

I grimace. "If you had to bet your life on my answer, what would you say?"

She smirks, a really good, Lilah Love quality smirk, and asks, "Pumpkin?"

"Don't be a bitch. I'm not in a good mood."

"Neither am I," she replies. "You cops closed off the street. No one is here to tip tonight."

"I'm not a cop."

She motions to the badge hanging around my neck. "Close enough. You have to order something other than coffee if you want to take up space."

I glance around the diner and then at her. "Because you're so damn busy?"

"You ordering or not?" Donna snaps back.

I pull out a twenty and slap it on the table. "That's my order."

"That'll get you a nice Pumpkin latte." She turns and walks away.

"Bitch!" I yell.

She lifts her hand and waggles her fingers at me. Damn, I think I like this woman. I chuckle to myself and then scan the street, but I can't see shit for the rain. I grab my phone and dial Director Murphy. He answers on the first ring. "Agent Love, how did you do on your first New York City case under my new task force?"

My. He's so self-focused and of course, the boss, so whatever. I guess it is his task force. "I came," I say. "I saw, I investigated *one* dead woman. Where are the other two?"

"I assumed you'd have extracted that information from those in charge of the scene."

"They said you were mistaken. There's one woman. That's all."

"Agent Love," he drawls, "what do you know about me?"

Besides his prickly bitch attitude, I think. He was with my mother while she was with my asshole of a father. He loved my mother. He believes she was murdered by Pocher and his Society, the same Society launching my father's political career. Oh, and he doesn't make mistakes. "Roger told you three women and a serial killer."

"Yes, and it's interesting that he would tell you otherwise. Perhaps Roger was willing to give up control to the FBI but Detective Williams was trying to keep your role as a consultant only."

"Perhaps, but I can tell you right now that Detective Williams is a f—joke." I leave out the word fucking because he's my boss. I also skip over my extreme desire to bitch slap a bitch, because he's also a director. I can be professional like that, if forced. "That crime scene was a mess," I add instead. "I wanted to claim jurisdiction, but, of course, we have no grounds to do so. And for the record, Roger Griffin doesn't call in help. He is the help. This smells bad."

"I'm certain you're resourceful enough to call Roger Griffin and take this where it leads."

I grimace at this suggestion that may or may not be innocent, but I wonder if he knows I'm avoiding Roger. Murphy's smart. He's observant. This man seems to know things about me that he shouldn't know, and he pushes my buttons. He pushes me to prove myself for reasons I don't even understand, and this has me thinking back to just last week when I'd agreed to join this task force.

"I want what you want," he says.

35

"Which is what?" I ask.

"The wrong people who are presently in power, out of power. You'll work for me, but live in Manhattan. You'll be part of a task force that I'm being assigned to head up. Together, we'll solve cold cases around the country, but you'll be assigned to the New York state region since it's your home turf. You'll consult locally and still travel to aid other regions if your skills are needed."

"And this does what for me and you?"

"In time, that will be clear. For now, you keep your badge and my protection, but you'll reside and work in New York state."

"Agent Love."

I blink back to the present. "What aren't you telling me about this case?" I ask.

"What haven't *you* told *me*, Agent Love?" he counters.

There's a part of me that doesn't trust this man, perhaps the part that doesn't like how much he seems to know about me and my family, even more, it seems, at times, than I do. "There might be a situation we need to discuss. Right now, I can't say. I'm working the case. That means I know very little."

"Very little," he says. "That's not very impressive."

"Yet," I add.

"Then it seems you need to make a phone call. Get your answers and then communicate, Agent Love. You're deficient in that area as this call proves once again." He disconnects.

Donna sets a cup of coffee in front of me with whipped cream on top. I grab a spoon and scoop up some of the sweet cream. I might not like the pumpkin that I'm certain is beneath it, but sugar, sugar is good to me. Of course, I'm putting off the inevitable in the call that Murphy expects me to make. He really does seem to be testing me, trying to see if I can really handle taking on the Society. They had me raped. I could kill them all and be happy, but maybe that's the point. If I want to keep this job, I have to be better at pretending I'm like everyone else.

36

"Damn you, Murphy," I mumble as I pick up the ridiculous pumpkin coffee. My lips find the lip of the white mug, and I take a swig, grimacing with the odd spicy taste of pumpkin. I set said ridiculous pumpkin coffee back down and pluck another twenty out of my pocket and slap it onto the table.

Donna laughs from behind the counter, a deep amused chuckle. "Plain coffee coming up."

I return my attention to the call I need to make. If I drank that nasty ass coffee, I can call my old mentor. It's not like he's going to look into my eyes over the phone and see what I've become. He won't know that I'm not like everyone else. He won't know how easily I can kill. Only Kane knows. Only Kane understands. I inhale and dial a number, but it's not Roger that I call: it's fucking Kane.

"Ah, beautiful," he murmurs in that deep rich voice of his. "Finally, you call me back. We're making progress. You actually *did* call me back."

"When are you coming back?"

"Miss me?"

"Kane," I warn.

"Lilah?"

"That problem you thought you solved; it's not solved."

He'll know what I mean. He'll know that I'm talking about the Society because here's the thing about the man I both love and hate: he dangerous and he's smart. "I'm coming back now."

"Okay."

"Okay?"

"Yes," I say. "Okay."

"Holy fuck. You never say okay."

"Maybe I know when to call in a drug kingpin."

"I'm not a fucking drug kingpin. I am not my fucking father."

And yet, Kane sure used that connection to back Pocher off when he thought the man was going to kill me. "You never say okay," he repeats. "What do I need to know right now?"

37

"To come back. That's all right now. And for the record, the next time I don't say okay, you should fucking listen because, clearly, it means I *don't* need help."

"Are you really taking this moment in time to lecture me about being protective?"

"No. I'm taking this moment in time to lecture you about being overbearing and intrusive."

"That's not what you said last night," he refutes.

"Kane," I warn again.

"Where are you?"

"In a diner, watching the crime scene I just left."

He doesn't ask questions, but I know Kane, and he knows me. He'll read between the lines. That crime scene led to this call. "I'll call you back once I make arrangements. And I'm sending someone to look after you."

"If you do, you'll pay the price."

He lowers his voice. "I do love the way you do angry sex, Lilah."

"Kane, if you send someone to watch me, and I mistake them for a problem, I will shoot them."

"Then I'll send someone I don't mind losing."

He hangs up.

CHAPTER SIX

I don't bother to call Kane back. We fight each other, and everyone else, better in person.

I take another drink of the pumpkin concoction in the white mug, and lord help me, maybe it's not that bad. Either way, I'm not becoming a seasonal pumpkin groupie. It's gingerbread or nothing for me. And it's this phone call and walk down memory lane with my old mentor or nothing for me. Murphy made that clear.

I tab through my contacts to find Roger Griffin's number. I haven't spoken to this man in years. I don't know why I still have his number, but I do, and I'm using it now. I have no choice. That crime scene was staged for me, and he knows how that originated. I have to know why he called me in on this one. I punch the damn Call button and hold my breath.

"Roger Griffin here," he answers in his gravelly smoker's voice, and the fact that he doesn't know who's calling—I never gave him my LA number—gives me just a minute to picture him, sun and smoke damaged, behind his old wooden desk. The one he used to have me sit at across from him, while he made me analyze a case, just before he told me to try again but do it right this time. And I did.

"Hello?" he says.

"It's Lilah."

"Lilah Love?" He sounds shocked, which is ten kinds of off since he's the one who called me to this crime scene.

"Yes. Yes, it's me. Long time no talk."

"Ya think? Crazy. I *just* watched a movie with your mother in it the other night, back when she went blonde to play Marilyn Monroe. I can't get my head around her being gone, not that I ever had the pleasure of meeting her, but seeing her on screen and knowing she's gone, I can't imagine how that makes you feel."

Oh, stop fucking talking, I think. Stop. He takes me back
to Ted Pocher's billion-dollar tell-all comment when I ran
into him at my father's house last week: *You remind me of
your mother a little more than I thought.* In other words,
I'm a problem to be disposed of, and if not for his fear of
Kane, I'd probably be dead right now. Pocher would be dead
right now, too, if not for Kane. Kane and I need to have a
conversation about that topic.

"Even with that brown hair of yours," he continues. "you
look just like her. It's uncanny. Of course, you're a gruff,
rough cussing machine. Hard to imagine that on-screen
beauty saying fuck all the time. Anyway, watching her had
me thinking about you and here you are calling."

"I was actually shocked to get called into this case
tonight," I add, moving on, "and even more so when you
weren't there."

"What case?" He coughs that smoker's cough of his, and
I can almost see his weathered skin, dark and wrinkled.
"Wait," he adds, clearing his throat. God, I hate the way he
clears his throat, to the point that I can't even allow myself
to describe it in my mind. "Are you here in New York?"

"Yes. Of course, I'm here. I'm confused. I thought you
knew? I was called to a crime scene tonight at your request."

"Not at my request. I'm in Connecticut doing a law
enforcement consultation. Maybe someone heard you were
in New York and decided to get you on the scene, which was
smart. I trained you right and all."

My fingers thrum on the table, and Donna sets a coffee
carafe and cup beside me, filling it with steaming hot brew.
I guess I finally tipped her enough to get what I wanted. "You
didn't call me in?" I ask, glancing out at the rain that just
keeps falling and with it, more shit. The shit just keeps
coming.

"Not me. Definitely not me."

"My boss was told that you called and that there were
three female victims and a serial killer on the loose that you
were having trouble catching up with on your own."

He snorts. "You ever known me to call in back up? And, you know how damn much serial killers intrigue me; I wouldn't give that one up."

No. No, he would not. I knew that.

"Is that what you got on your hands?" he asks. "A serial killer?"

"I don't know enough to confirm anything at this point. I have one dead female who was posed by the asshole who killed her."

"One victim, not three? Didn't I hear you say three?"

"The detective on the case insists this is a singular case. Williams. Do you know her?"

"Yeah. Piece of work that one." He doesn't elaborate, moving on to the puzzle. He loves the puzzle. He always told me to work the problem you can solve. "Where the hell did the number three come from?" he asks.

"Where did the call come from?" I counter. "My boss really believes he spoke to you."

"That was a mix up of some sort. He didn't speak to me, and I'm here for a bit now. I've got two dead women in two weeks."

One plus two equals three. "Posed?" I ask.

"Yes, posed."

"Any props?"

"High heels," he says. "This one likes high heels. You think mine and yours equal the three?"

"Mine was posed with an umbrella."

"Hair color?"

"Blonde," I say.

"Mine are brunette," he says. "Age?"

"Late twenties."

"Thirties here. It doesn't sound like a match."

And yet, I repeat in my mind, one plus two equals three, and someone wanted me to connect the dots that lead to him. "Can we trade case files?"

"Considering you're working what should be my case, yes. It's way past time we solved a case together, kiddo. Text me a secure email address."

"Will do."

"And Roger, this feels off. You need to be careful. I can approve protection—"

"Hell no. If some killer finally gets this old man, I'll go out doing what I love to do."

"You aren't the guy that fights off a criminal and shoots them. You profile them."

"I can handle a gun and myself, woman. Enough."

He hangs up.

I tried, and I leave it at that. I shift back to the case, processing what I know. I'm really not sure if this is the Society or a straight up killer fucking with me. My gaze lifts to the window in hopes of a view of the crime scene, in hopes that a light bulb will turn on and answers will follow. What I find is a person in a trench coat holding a red umbrella, blocking my view. There are *no coincidences*. This is not an accident. Adrenaline surges with the certainty that I'm being fucked with all over again, taunted, even baited to go outside. Most people would say don't go, but I'm not most people. My hand goes to my weapon, and I stand up and head for the door.

CHAPTER SEVEN

I don't actually pull my gun. Not with Donna around, not because I'm afraid of scaring Donna, but because I wouldn't put it past her to chuck a coffee pot at me. No. My hand shoves up the hem of my hoodie that I'm wearing over my holster, and I grip my weapon, ready for a quick pull and discharge should it become necessary. I exit to the sidewalk, and the umbrella is gone. Any sign of a human on this side of the street is gone. My own umbrella, that wasn't my umbrella at all, is also gone. The rain, not fucking gone at all.

I could run out into the rain chasing a ghost while amusing some asshole watching, or I could go back inside and drink my pumpkin latte. I go back inside the diner and sit down, waving to Donna. "More whipped cream. Oh hell. Just bring me another latte." I slap another bill on the table. I'm done shying away from my family money. I'm done pretending I'm not my mother's daughter. That was all about forgetting things I no longer want to forget. I want to remember. I want the Society to know that I fucking remember.

Donna arches a brow from behind the counter. "You want another pumpkin latte? Are you serious?"

"Just bring the damn latte," I say, dialing Jeff, otherwise known as Tic Tac, my go-to tech guy back at the bureau in LA, the city where half my belongings still preside though I do not. And as for that nickname, I don't know why we call him that, but it irritates him; therefore, I like it.

"Lilah," he answers because, unlike Roger, Tic Tac knows my number. "I just want to start this conversation by saying that I will not secretly help you behind Director Murphy's back, literally behind his back. He's back in LA, you know? His office is around the corner from mine. I will not get fired."

I might have gotten him in a little trouble recently, but Murphy got over it. "Eat a donut," I say. "We both know that's your comfort food. And then take some notes. I need stuff."

"I am eating a donut. I'm at Hurts Donuts with *a date*. And you don't work for the LA division anymore."

"But I work for Murphy. Call him. He'll confirm, and then we can actually get some work done."

He sighs. "Text me what you need."

"You don't have your computer with you?"

"Date, Lilah. I'm *on a date*."

"And I have a dead woman. She was blonde. Pretty. Her whole life before her that is now gone. She was naked with an umbrella posed in her hand, but get this, the blood that was in the Tupperware container that was attached to the ceiling fan before it was turned on was someone else's."

"Thank you, Lilah, for ruining my donut." He murmurs to someone else, a muffled tone now, but I still hear him say, "Hold on, Mike. Just one more minute."

"Mike?" I ask incredulously. "You're on a date with Mike?"

"Yeah, Lilah. You ruined women for me. Happy?"

"I didn't ruin women for you. You were born that way. If I inspired you to embrace the real you then you owe me a donut."

"Just text me the information," he snaps. "We're going to leave and head to my place."

"There's a connection to that problem we've been dealing with, so be careful."

"Another dead woman and a connection to *them*. Wonderful." He hangs up.

Donna sets my coffee in front of me along with a slice of pumpkin pie. "Try it." She points to the whipped cream on top. "I added that just for you."

"Fine, but you're still a bitch. Get something other than pumpkin in this place."

She smirks and walks away. She likes me, too. I take a bite of the pie. Yep, it's pumpkin, but my taste buds have temporarily accepted this as their evening fate. I begin my text message to Tic Tac, sharing everything I can on an open line:

Roger Griffin. Is he really in Connecticut? When did he get there? I need details on the case he's presently working. Actually, I need a complete history but focus on the past year. Next. The woman is Mia Moore. Twenty-eight. Former model turned advertising executive. Get me everything you can on her and her family, love life, you know. All that shit you dig up for me. The detective running the case is a woman, last name Williams. I need to know all about her, too. More soon.

He doesn't reply. He must be sucking face with Mike and trying to make this alright with him. I sympathize, but there are lives on the line. Oh crap. I have a thought. I dial Tic Tac again. "Lilah. You do know I have to drive to get to my computer, right?"

"I left out details that I can't put in a text. It's too much."

"No kidding?"

"Murphy got a call tonight that was supposedly from Roger Griffin asking for me on this crime scene. Roger says that call didn't come from him. We need to know who called Murphy."

"I am not hacking my boss' phone."

"It's possible that a serial killer called your boss and may well think he'd make a tasty treat. We need to know who contacted Murphy and said they were Roger."

"I'm calling Murphy," he growls.

"Good. Then I don't have to." This time, I hang up.

I sigh and consider leaving the diner, but the storm just *won't* let up. Instead, I finish off my pie and coffee, and by the time I'm done, finally, the rain has eased to a sprinkle. It's also one in the morning, and my view of the crime scene across the street is now blocked by a blue plastic wall that's been put up. I'd like to think that it's to protect the evidence, but I believe it's more about staying dry.

I slip in my earbuds to free my hands for a walk home, stand up, and wave at Donna. "Get some damn strawberry pie, and I'll be back."

"Well, as long as it gets *you* back, we'll get the strawberry pie. We'll change up the whole menu for the likes of you."

"Smartass. I'm a good tipper." I don't wait for a reply. I slip on my jacket and then pull up the hood. Wasting no time, I step outside and walk toward my apartment.

I've just gotten past the barricades, that weren't present before, when the prickling at the back of my neck begins. I'm being watched, and I don't like it. My hand shifts under my jacket, lifting my hoodie, settling on my gun. This could be Kane's man and lord knows this isn't the first time he's had me followed, but I'm on edge. I don't like what I feel.

My cellphone rings, and I grab it from my pocket to find Kane's number on my caller ID. "What's happening?" he asks when I answer.

"There was a dead body posed with an umbrella with someone else's blood in a Tupperware container attached to a ceiling fan."

"And?"

And this man knows me. Those details don't equal me asking him to return. "Murphy got a call from Roger requesting me on this crime scene, but Roger didn't make the call. If that isn't enough, Beth was called in as well. Beth who only works in Long Island. If *that's* not enough, the scene was staged for me."

"Staged meaning what?"

"I found two Marlboro cigarettes."

"Roger's brand."

"I'm not going to ask how you know that."

"I make it a point of knowing everyone in your life, beautiful."

"If this didn't mean you know things I now need to know about Roger, I'd remind you that you qualify as a stalker."

"I protect what's mine," he says as I pass an alleyway and feel something, really fucking feel something.

"I'm not yours," I say, but I stop walking.

"Lilah—"

"Wait," I warn softly, and I turn to the dark as fuck alleyway.

46

It's not empty. Standing there, under a beam of a lone light, as if in a spotlight, is a woman, in a dress and heels, holding an umbrella. "Oh fuck," I murmur.

"What does that mean?" Kane demands. "Lilah what does 'oh fuck' mean and where are you?"

I can't listen to him in my ear right now. I disconnect the call, and for the third time in an hour, reach for my weapon.

CHAPTER EIGHT

Kane immediately tries to call me back, and I swear I'd rip those earbuds out of my ear if I dared use my hand for anything but the Glock I'm now holding. The woman—or the person dressed as a woman, I can't be sure in the shit show of a wet, dark alleyway—doesn't move. I ease forward, and the rain decides to be a perfect little bitch by way of a torrential downpour again. The ringing in my ear stops only to start again. I'm going to throttle Kane when I see him. Or shoot him. I really think I need to shoot someone tonight.

With my weapon in front of me, finger on the trigger, I reach in my bag and grab a flashlight, and holy fuck, I can't seem to put my hand on it. Screw it, time is everything when a life is on the line—mine or someone else's—so I move toward the person holding that damn umbrella. It's a red umbrella just like the one I left by the diner door. Holy hell, she's holding the umbrella I left behind. And that umbrella is shaking. The closer I get, the more it seems to shake. I don't assume to know why. It could be fear. It could be part of a game.

"Hands in the air," I shout. "Drop the umbrella."

"I can't drop the umbrella!" a woman shouts, her voice muffled in the rain, but the desperation is there, raw and real. She's either a good actor or a victim. Hell, I've seen good actors play victims before. "It's glued to my hand!" she calls out. "Don't shoot! Don't shoot. Please don't shoot!"

It takes me a few seconds to fully process the implications of her words. Another second to decide that I hear real fear in her voice. And only one more to say fuck it and decide I'm gambling on this woman being the real deal. I'm risking my life to save this woman's life. The light that was shining on her goes off. That's my cue.

Running forward into the dark abyss of that alleyway, I close the space between me and the woman. The minute I reach her, I grab her, scanning the black hole beyond her with my gun raised, fighting the urge to shoot, because while I don't mind killing someone, I want to pick that someone. I don't trust the asshole behind all of this not to have another innocent woman standing there waiting for my bullet.

Still facing the unknown darkness, I place the woman's back to my back and start pushing her forward, out of the alley, keeping my gun on the unknown, expecting a threat to be launched at me at any moment. The woman starts screaming, reacting to something in front of her—holy fucking hell. I know this could be a trap—someone coming at me from both directions—but I do the only thing I can, what my instincts tell me to do.

I rotate and step in front of the woman, my gun aimed at whoever or whatever is making her scream. A man in a rain jacket stands there all but toe to toe with me now, his gun at his side, mine pointed at his chest. "I'm with Kane," he declares as the street light illuminates his sharp, high cheekbones. "I'm covering you." He doesn't wait for agreement. He cuts around us and damn if he doesn't bravely trek into the unknown.

"Help," the woman gasps from behind me. "Help."

I turn, and she falls to her knees toward me. I drop with her, holding her up and that damn umbrella slams into my back. I grunt through the pain. "Help," she gasps, her head falling forward onto my shoulder as she starts making gurgling sounds.

Poison. This is poison.

Aware of a ticking clock, I don't think about the risk to myself. Struggling with her weight, I lay her on her side, a position meant to open her airway and keep her from choking if she vomits, all but poking my eye out with the umbrella in the process. My phone rings again, and this time, I answer. "Lilah," Kane says urgently.

"Call 911," I order, already pulling a rubber glove from my bag. "Woman down," I add. "Possible poisoning. Now Kane. Now." He disconnects without asking for an address, but then he knows my location and thank God for it. I yank my soaked hood back from my soaked hair, and because I believe we're dealing with a toxin and my hand has to go into her mouth, I pull the glove onto my left hand. The gun stays in in my right, the hand that gives me the most accuracy, and somehow, I still manage to roll her onto her back before shoving my fingers into her mouth, searching for a foreign object.

"We're clear from the rear," Kane's man announces as he kneels beside me. "No way to get to you from there or above." His voice is heavily accented, an ugly scar ripped down his cheek, and I swear if he's from the cartel, I will thank them both and then beat them when this is over. "What the hell is the deal with the umbrella?" he asks.

"It's glued to her hands. Don't touch it. She's been poisoned. Don't make yourself next. I promised Kane I'd kill you myself." I pull my hand from her mouth. There's nothing there. There's nothing I can fix. I shove her back to her side. Sirens sound nearby, thank God, and with Kane's man present, I shove my gun in my holster and lean in to check the woman's breathing. She starts to convulse. I can't do anything but grab the umbrella with my gloved hand to keep it from hurting her. I can't even order Kane's man to hold her down without risking a toxin affecting him. As it is, I'm already exposed, but I'm the only one, and it needs to stay that way.

A beam of light flares down the alleyway, lights from a fire truck, and three firemen rush our way. "Agent Love, FBI," I call out, and as one of the men approaches, I quickly add, "I suspect a toxin, and this isn't a singular incident. Protect yourselves." The woman stops convulsing and goes stiff, no sounds coming from her mouth. "Fuck," I murmur, eyeing the fireman in front of me, my hands settling on my knees. "No obstruction in her mouth. That's all I know."

He nods, and I stand up, giving the other men joining him room to work. Rain starts to fall again. I'm not sure it ever stopped, but I don't have time to let it slow me down. The little bitch who did this is somewhere nearby. I hurry toward the street where I meet two police officers now approaching. I grab my badge and step in front of them, flashing it. "FBI. Agent Love. Possible toxin. Suspect on the loose. No description. Block off the street and start canvasing now. One of you get on the air now." I grab a baggie from my bag and use it to remove my glove and then hand it to one of the officers. "Evidence. Have it tested." I unzip my hoodie and let it fall to the ground. "That too. Use gloves."

One of the officers is already on his walkie talkie, ordering the barricades and the search. I turn to the other as two more officers and a fireman join us. The fireman is my focus. "We don't need anyone that isn't already active on scene. Protect your men. Send everyone you can back to the station." He nods and hurries away. I look at one of the officers. "You block off the alleyway and get a forensics team in here now." I look between them. "This is now a crime scene directly connected to the Mia Moore murder two blocks down. I'm taking control. Tell Detective Williams that if she wants to fight me on this to talk to my superior, Director Murphy. Understood?"

"Yes ma'am," one of the officers says, followed by the next, and everyone launches into action.

Someone brings me a police jacket that I accept. I'm pulling it on when Kane's man steps to my side, and I turn to him. "We need to figure out where the piece of shit who did this is right now. He or she is here. You go right. I'll go left."

"No," he says. "My orders are to stay with you."

"Two choices," I reply. "I have you arrested or you follow my orders."

He grimaces. "You live up to your bitch reputation."

"Thank you," I say, accepting the compliment. "Now go."

I glance behind me to find tape being pulled across the alleyway. That's all I need to see. I draw my weapon and my flashlight, heading down the street, a calm overtaking me. He wants to rattle me. He wants me to overreact, to do something stupid. Too bad he picked the wrong agent. I won't overreact. I won't arrest him. I'll kill him. I ease into the shadows, checking out every dark corner, looking up, right, left, behind, and forward. I pass law enforcement. I give orders. I give answers. I stop at alleyways and even dare to make tracks behind buildings. I'm not going to get the kill I crave tonight.

I return to the alleyway as Beth arrives and seeing her tells me what I'd already assumed. "She's dead," I say as we both step to the line of tape.

"Yes. She's dead. What the fuck, Lilah?" And this time, she doesn't say pardon my French. "There's two dead women now. I'm back to what is this?"

Two dead women.

The killer said there were three.

That means someone else is about to die.

CHAPTER NINE

Kane's man stalks toward Beth and me, clearly done with his search for Umbrella Man and ready to talk. A conversation I don't want to have with Beth present. "Don't leave without talking to me," I tell her, stepping away from her to motion my newest stalker off to the side under an overhang. I'm so done with rain right now and really, truly, I could shoot someone.

"Anything?" I ask.

He gives a grim shake of his head and pulls his hood down, his thick, dark hair soaked, that scar on his cheek ugly. "Nothing," he says, "but the bastard's here. I can feel him watching us."

He's right. Umbrella Man is watching. I feel him, too. And yes, he's a man. Every time I think of him, he's a man. I'd be willing to bet my badge on it. For now, I move on to the stranger before me. I don't like strangers, even when they're Kane's strangers. "Who are you?"

"Call me Jay," he says, which translates to that's not my real name.

"Who do you work for?"

"You know who I work for," he counters without missing a beat.

"Who is Kane to you?"

"My boss."

Now he's just trying to irritate me. "*Who is Kane to you?*" I press.

"A rich, powerful man. Who are *you* to Kane? Some might call you his weakness. I call you the trigger."

I don't ask what he means. I know. Kane would do anything for me, even kill. Some might think that's a romantic notion, but this is Kane Mendez we're talking about. He really would kill for me, and he'll feel no regret when it's done. I know this about him. I understand him, perhaps too well.

Irritated that this man is about to take me down a dangerous rabbit hole where Kane is concerned, I want him gone. "Make me think you disappeared," I say, already walking away, placing several feet between me and the general mass of law enforcement leaning on the germ-infested New York City wall next to a closed restaurant. I'm brave like that. I keep proving it over and over tonight.

Snatching my phone from my pocket, it's Kane that's on my mind, but I dial Director Murphy. Kane, I'll deal with when he gets back from one of his "don't ask any questions" kind of business trips that always piss me off.

"Agent Love," Murphy answers, alert and awake, despite what has to be the early morning hour at this point. "I hear you took jurisdiction. On what grounds?"

"That wasn't Roger Griffin who called you and requested me on that murder scene tonight. A scene no one in law enforcement connected to any other murders or a serial killer."

"If Griffin didn't call me, who did?"

"Considering the messages left for me at the crime scene, I'd say someone who wants to play cat and mouse with me."

"You think it was the killer."

"I know it was. He killed twice tonight. I was called to murder number one. He setup number two in an alleyway that I had to pass to get home, and then waited on me to find her."

"I heard. That's two women dead. The caller said three. Is there a known third?"

"Technically," I say, as realization hits me, "we only have two murders, however, the initial crime scene had an excess of blood that didn't belong to the victim. I suspect the owner of that blood is the third victim."

"That would mean the crimes don't fit a pattern. Two suspected poisonings, from what I understand with no blood loss. The third being a completely different kind of kill."

I consider that but not for long. "Oh fuck. I mean—"

"Speak freely, Agent Love."

"The blood was mimicking rain. He didn't need blood for the second woman. He had rain."

"I see. Interesting. A reasonable assumption I doubt few would immediately conclude, but does that mean we have two or three victims?"

"He's a drama queen. He wouldn't miss the chance to claim a kill. Three. We have three murders but that doesn't mean he won't stage more."

"Agreed. What do you need from me?"

"Beth Smith was called to the scene, too. She's—"

"The coroner who worked the cases with you that connected to our dear friends."

"Is that what we're calling them now?" I ask because I know good and well that he means the Society. Beth and I literally just wrapped up an investigation of a series of assassinations that were directly linked to the Society covering up their existence. Assassinations pinned on someone close to my father, but not so close as to screw up his Society-sponsored run for New York governor.

"On an open line, yes, Agent Love. They are our dear friends. That's what we're calling them. In person, we'll speak frankly, preferably in your language."

"I'm speaking that language in my head right now."

"And I can hear you," he assures me. "Is Beth's situation linked to the killer's game or our dear friends?"

"I don't know, but she looks like the victims. Is this all a staged threat by our 'dear friends' or is a killer just playing with me? Either way, I'm worried about her."

"Consider that problem solved."

"How?" I press.

"You'll know when it happens. I'll remove her from reach."

"Soon," I press.

"Immediately," he assures me. "What else can I do to help right now?"

"Tic Tac—"

"Is at your disposal."

"I told him to look into that Griffin call you received."

"As you should have. And he told me. What else, Agent Love?"

My brows dip. "Why exactly are you being so agreeable?"

"Because, for once, you're communicating. It works. Keep making it work. What else?"

He's such a smartass and the only way to handle a smartass is by being a bigger smartass. "I'll communicate if I need anything."

"Excellent decision. I'm going to bed. Tic Tac's also in bed, Agent Love. Let him sleep. I'll tell him to contact you after noon your time." He disconnects.

I dial Tic Tac. He answers on the first ring. "Director Murphy said you'd be calling me."

Of course he did. He knew I'd call even when he told me not to call. I'm perhaps becoming too predictable for my own good. "Just give me what I need to know. Did Old Man Smokey make the call to Murphy?" I ask, giving Roger an overdue nickname though Gruff Old Fuck might be more appropriate.

"If you mean Roger Griffin, I can't say. The call came in from a number assigned to a disposable phone that I traced back to Brooklyn. And before you ask, no, I don't know who bought it. That store's been closed for five years."

"I'm too tired right now to even say fuck to that with proper emphasis." And I don't even know why this question keeps coming to mind, but I need the answer. "Is Old Man Smokey in Connecticut?"

"Yes."

"And he got there when?"

"Per his hotel and travel arrangements, last night."

I should feel relief that Smokey is telling the truth, but I don't. The killer is watching him, the killer knew where he was and planned tonight's events accordingly, but also on a rainy night. That just seems like a damn near impossible feat. "Is there anything else I need to know right now?"

"Is there anything else you *want* to know? Yes. Is there anything else you *need* to know right now before we all sleep? No."

Suddenly a laser to a gun is pointed at my chest. I freeze, and damn it, my heart starts to race, a reaction I don't like to give any piece of shit killer. "Lilah?"

At Tic Tac's prodding, I decide that I can't alert him to my present shit circumstances without risking a trap that ends with someone else being shot. "Go to bed," I order.

"I don't need to be told twice." He hangs up.

The minute he disconnects, I decide that if this entire situation is a staged event by the Society to scare me then fuck them. If they want to kill me, then I'm already dead. If this is a crazy fucker and a serial killer, he wants to play, which means he won't kill me. I lift my hands and fire off two middle fingers in the direction of the laser. It immediately disappears. I push off the wall and start walking back toward the rest of my crew. The laser doesn't reappear and sending someone chasing its location will be futile. The asshole who pointed it at me gets a game point but not a win.

Beth is waiting on me when I arrive back to the alley, huddling deeper into a NYPD jacket and shivering. "What don't I know?"

"You know nothing, Beth Smith," I say in my best Ygritte *Game of Thrones'* voice and accent.

She glares at me. "Did you really just make a *Game of Thrones* joke at a murder scene?"

"Yep. Sure did. And you got the joke. *You* watch *Game of Thrones*?"

"What I get is that I worry about you sometimes. How can you go through this hell tonight and joke around?"

"Should I cry? I've practiced that for certain situations. Would you like to see?"

She positively glowers. "Lilah—"

"I want you to stay at a high-end hotel for a few days, one with lots of security until I get you reassigned out of town for a while. I'll pay."

Her eyes go wide. "You think I need to leave town?"

"Yes. I do."

"I—God—holy hell. I don't need the hotel. I've got a new man, believe it or not. I'm officially dating an FBI agent here in the city. I'm staying with him. I'll be safe for now."

This news delivers a laundry list of possibilities:

1) I know from working with Murphy that the local FBI has a connection to Pocher and the Society. That could confirm that this is all indeed a way for the Society to keep me busy and remind me how easily they can hurt those I love.

2) Her boyfriend got her on this job to be closer to her.

3) Her boyfriend is the Umbrella Man.

Not to mention she wasn't dating him two weeks ago, when she told me she was destined to be single forever. I frown. "What's his name?"

"Jess Monroe. Do you know him?"

"No," I say, but I wonder if he knows me.

I'm sure about to know him, especially since I don't know how to keep her away from him. "I'll still get you a room at the Ritz. Take him with you. I'd feel better if you were in a controlled situation."

"You're that worried?"

I've never been one to sugarcoat things, and when I try, it usually goes badly. I don't even try now. "I'll book the room."

She makes a face, and I'm pretty sure she might cry. Crying requires coddling, and I don't do well with coddling, mostly because it often forces you to lie. I'm not going to lie to Beth. "I'll text you the reservation," I say and walk away.

And since I can't assign law enforcement when she's with law enforcement, I then text Kane: *Have "Jay" follow Beth.*

He replies with: *Done. Can you talk?*

I reply with: *In person.*

He doesn't push. He understands what I'm telling him. There are things to say, but they can't be spoken on an open phone line.

Next, I text Tic Tac: *FBI agent Jess Monroe. I need to know everything about him. If we miss something, someone might die.*

He replies with: *You really do know how to ruin a guy's life, Lilah Love.*

Maybe I do, but if I save Beth's, I can live with that.

***

Victim number two is identified, Shelly Willit, twenty-eight, and a literary editor. Age and hair color match that of Mia Moore, career might have a creative connection but a loose one; an advertising executive and an editor. It could be some connection to a book they both promoted. I bank that idea for later use. For now, it's Otherworld, crime scene mode. I do a walk through of Shelly's apartment that is only a few blocks from Mia's, directing the team in their efforts, but for me, on the surface, only one thing standing out. It's so clean she has to be OCD. Beyond all else, that could be the connecting dots. Two women, both OCD. She also likes books, she has lots of books, which makes sense, she's an editor but each is perfectly lined up. Each is completely dust free.

It's ten in the morning when I drag my drenched and dried mess of an ass into my apartment building. I could have been home at eight, but somehow, I fell asleep at a desk in the morgue, and some guy thought I was dead and started screaming. Despite taking a shower at the morgue—yes, they have a shower—and then dressing in a T-shirt and a pair of police pants, I'm pretty sure his reaction confirms that my version of looking like shit right now has reached epic proportions. I'm awake now, though, and ready to shower properly, drink coffee, eat something with ten thousand grams of sugar, and get to work.

Once I'm at my door on the fifteenth floor, I unlock it to find a tall, dark drink of trouble and hot man standing in the doorway. Kane is here, in my apartment, despite the fact that I haven't given him a key or security clearance to enter.

CHAPTER TEN

His strong square jaw is set hard, his favored Italian suit traded for a pair of black jeans and a T-shirt, his dark hair slicked back. He stands here in *my* apartment with me in the hallway, acting like he owns more than the moment, like he owns me. Kane is *that* arrogant. In fact, he personifies that damn word, so much so that those rich brown eyes of his burn me with their intensity, a dare in their depths. A dare to tell the lie I always want to tell when it comes to this man. He's daring me to say that I don't want him. He's daring me to say that I don't want him here. We both know that I do, of course, want him and want him here. Wanting Kane, wanting him in my life, has never been the problem. All the parts of us that are the same in that dark dirty way, that feed more of the same in each other, those things are the problem.

He says I pull him toward the right.

I say he pulls me toward the wrong.

He says we land in the middle.

I'm afraid the middle is still a dangerous place.

I don't like to feel fear.

Anger comes at me hard and fast and from a deep simmering place. I pull my gun and stalk toward him. He backs up, moving deeper into the apartment with me following. "Holy fuck, Lilah. Are we really doing this again?"

I kick my door shut. I even take the time to lock my door because I don't want to get killed by Umbrella Man while killing Kane. "I didn't invite you in. I told you not to have Jay stalk me."

"Lilah," he warns softly. "You pulling a gun on me is getting old."

"What are you going to do about it? Kill me? I'm the one with the fucking gun."

He moves, and he's fast, athletic, a black belt who taught me to be a black belt. He catches my hand, closing his over

63

mine and the weapon, but we both know I let him. He doesn't even try to take it from me. He steps closer into the barrel and presses it against his chest. "Shoot me this time or stop pointing a gun at me. Now or never, beautiful."

"You think I won't do it?"

"I know you and what you will and won't do. I know you like no one else knows you and that pisses you off. You're a killer, Lilah, of course you'll do it, but to be clear, it's the only way you'll get rid of me."

The root of my anger explodes into reality, burning through me, and I don't even try to hold it back. "Seems like you were pretty easy to get rid of all those years that I was in LA."

"You know why I didn't come after you."

"Because you were too busy fucking that blonde bimbo in the Hamptons?"

"Holy fuck, Lilah. I'm a man. I had sex. I was fucking here. You were all but living with Rich."

"Rich was a co-worker I happened to fuck in LA."

"Who came here and went after me? Because he was *just* a fuck buddy? Bullshit. He wanted to marry you."

"And I should have married him. He was good for me."

"And I'm not?"

"We're not good for each other."

Now anger flares in *his* eyes. "Then fucking shoot me, Lilah. Deal with it once and for all. The Society would cheer my loss."

My cold heart isn't so cold with those words. The idea of this man gone hurts. It hurts bad. "Don't say that. I don't fucking want you dead, Kane. Let go of the gun."

"Are you going to stop pointing it at me?"

"Probably."

"Lilah—"

"I have anger issues with you, Kane. I hate you."

He stares at me a few beats and then releases my hand. He doesn't back away. I don't back away.

I stare down at the gun and then look at him. "It was easier when I didn't hate you."

He takes the gun and slides it into my holster. His hand settles on my hip, scorching in every possible way, in the certainty that I can't let him go, in the certainty that we will burn alive and do it together. He steps into me. "I stayed away to keep them away." He tangles his fingers in my hair and stares down at me. "Because I knew that if we were together, they'd see trouble. They'd come at you, and you weren't mentally ready for that. I did everything I did, including what I did when you were attacked, to protect you. Because I fucking love you, Lilah."

"And yet, every time I think about you staying away, that doesn't compute."

"There's no in between for us. It's all or nothing. That's who we are together. The minute I came for you, there would be no walking away without you. And you weren't ready for what that meant. You knew then, what we both know now. The only way for me to protect you is for me to kill them all."

I don't jolt with shock. This is Kane. This is the Kane I know. "Is that what you plan to do? Kill them all?"

"This is one of those moments when we both pretend that I didn't say what I just said. When we both pretend it doesn't mean what it means. But I don't lie to you. I have never lied to you. So I'm going to ask you now, with that in mind, do you really want me to answer that?"

"Yes. Answer, Kane. Is that your plan? To kill them all?"

"Yes, Lilah. I'm going to kill them all. I negotiated with Pocher and made you vow to back off to buy time, to do it right. Now you know. Now what?"

I blanch. "You told me the truth," I say stunned.

"*I never lied to you.*"

"Avoidance *is* a lie."

"You're lying to yourself if you think we don't walk around things together, that I do it alone. But let's go there, Lilah. Let's talk about lies."

"What does that even mean?"

"At least I'm willing to admit I need you. You need me, too, and every time you say you don't, you do what you hate; you lie to me and us. You lie to yourself. Are you going to keep telling that lie?"

Emotion that no one but this man makes me feel punches me in the chest, and I don't even try to name them all because what they are isn't the point. That they exist is. I don't feel much except with him. I feel a lot with him, so damn much, but some of those things aren't good. He buried a body for me when I was drugged. He made a decision for me that made me like him. Or maybe I was already like him and I just want to blame him? He catches my hair and forces my gaze to his. "Are you going to keep telling that lie, Lilah?"

"The truth is that I hate you."

"And you love me or I wouldn't be here, but you don't have to say it. Just show me. Show me now." And then his mouth is on my mouth, and there are a million reasons to push him away, but one very important reason not to: I just don't want to.

CHAPTER ELEVEN

"You scared the holy hell out of me last night," Kane hisses, dragging his mouth from mine, staring down at me. "If I would have lost you, I would have burned the damn city down. I would have kept burning cities down. You don't get to die, Lilah. Do you understand?"

This is one of those moments where Kane and I understand each other. It's one of those moments that all the times he has me followed, that he damn near stalks me make sense. His parents are dead, his mother was murdered over his father's business. Ironically, I now believe my mother fell to a similar fate. It's just one more of so many things that draws me to this man. "Just kiss me again already," I order, because I can't tell him that I won't die. He knows this. I know he knows this. I'm many things, but I'm not a liar. I won't make a promise I can't keep.

But he doesn't kiss me. He tightens his grip in my hair. He pushes me for more. "Say you understand, Lilah."

Suddenly, I realize that he isn't asking me to promise I won't die. He's asking me to understand why he makes the decisions he makes, but I can't do that when those decisions reach beyond having me followed. "You don't get a pass on all the bad things you do to protect me, Kane."

He murmurs something I can't make out in Spanish and then adds, "Lilah, damn it." But he doesn't push me again. This time, he kisses me, and this time, all the anger that was mine minutes before is now his. No, ours. We're both angry. We're both in a dark place, in a demanding place and for a reason. We have always fit together, two pieces of a two-piece puzzle, but our worlds haven't.

I press my hands under his shirt and shove it up. He reaches over his head and pulls it away and comes back for mine. He tosses it aside, and when he discovers my wet bra was long ago discarded, he makes this rough sound low in his throat that I've missed so damn badly. There are so many things about this man I've missed.

He catches my leg and then he's lifting me. I not only let him, but I pretty much climb all over him. I don't even care that he clearly knows my new bedroom is upstairs when he's never been here before today. It's clear that while he waited on me, he looked around, but I just don't care. I let him walk up the stairs without one word of objection. He enters my bedroom, bright sunlight peering through the floor-to-ceiling windows. I punch the button inside the door on the wall, and the shades begin to slide close. Kane walks straight for the chair and sits down, taking me with him.

This is another one of those moments when I know this man. This might seem like him giving me control, and he is, but it's not that simple with Kane. Kane can be dominant. Kane can take control, but he wants, even needs to know that I'm choosing him and us. In that need is both a power play and vulnerability. If he gets what he wants, if I show him how willingly I am here with him, I can no longer shove that gun between us and use it as an emotional divider. If I don't give him what he wants, I hurt him.

Every part of me is one hundred percent present in the moment with this man. I sink into the chair, my knees at his hips, my mouth pressed to his mouth. He holds me close, touches me, drinks me in, and when I push off of him and take his hand, urging him to his feet, he doesn't hesitate. We finish undressing, and there's a simmering heat between us that explodes when he drags me to him. He kisses me again, pulling me into his lap as he sits back down. He lifts me, and in one long thrust, he's inside me, and my fingers are pressed to his shoulders.

His eyes meet mine, and I see the flare of possessiveness in their depths, feel this man's power, and I don't know why, but for a moment, I'm back in time drugged and covered in blood, sitting in a bathtub, waiting as he cleaned up my mess. I knew he was taking care of my mess, but I blamed him for doing so; I've blamed him for years for forcing that secret on me, for not calling the police.

But some part of me now admits that he was protecting my badge. That he was protecting me from me even as I tried to convince myself I needed to be protected from him. I don't have the words to tell him, so I kiss him again, and for the next few minutes, I show him. When it's over, we end up in the bed under the blankets, both of us desperate for sleep with me willingly pressed close to him.

"You might not like who you are outside of that badge, Lilah," he says after several minutes, "but who you are isn't that badge. I know you feel like you're more like me than you want to be and that I'm more like my father than I should be, but it can't save you from yourself or from me."

He's always wanted to let it go. He's always felt it was a wall between us. "What if it's the only thing saving us both?"

LISA RENEE JONES

CHAPTER TWELVE

Kane doesn't answer that question. I didn't really expect him to either. On some level, we both know we need my badge to keep us grounded. On some level, we both know my badge will always divide us, but I'm ready to see it in a new way. Not so long ago, I threw my badge away, and Kane convinced me that was a mistake. He insisted that I need the badge, *we* need the badge. I believe that me wearing it influences his decisions. We're both pulled to the dark side. We're both able to justify a means to the right end. This doesn't bother Kane at all. It does me. Without the badge, would I become more like him? That's the last thought I have before I do what I once thought I'd never do again: fall asleep pressed close to Kane fucking Mendez.

I have no idea how long I sleep, but I wake to the ringing of my phone that is plugged in on the nightstand. With a groan of disapproval, I roll over and grab it, glancing at the clock that reads two in the afternoon, which means I've had all of two hours of sleep. A good reason to ignore this caller if it wasn't Beth. "Why the hell aren't you sleeping?" I ask. "They have good beds at the Ritz."

"I woke up with a nightmare: me with one of those damn umbrellas over my head. I just realized why you're worried about me. I look like them. The women who this monster killed. I *look like them.* How did I not get that last night? My God, Lilah. What aren't you telling me?"

I sit up and Kane sits with me, arching an eyebrow in my direction. I mouth "she's scared," and he nods, understanding in that one little action. We're getting up. Last night's hell is already visiting today. In unison, we each turn to our side of the bed and swing our legs off the edge. "I mean my God," Beth continues. "How could you not warn me?" she presses.

"I have someone watching out for you," I assure her, looking around for Kane's shirt to pull over me. I'm fine with my nudity but somehow being naked and talking to Beth feels weird. "And," I add, giving up on the shirt and focusing on just calming her down, "this someone will shoot first and ask questions later."

"Oh God. Kane. You got Kane involved?"

The rumors about Kane are all over that statement, and I purse my lips, fighting protectiveness for a man who doesn't need or likely even deserve my protection. "Yes, but—"

"Thank you. Thank you so much. I'm going to work. I need to catch this fucker."

"Fucker?" I ask in disbelief because Beth comes from a refined family, and unlike me, she actually uses the manners she was taught.

"Yes. This fucker doesn't get to win. I'll be there in an hour."

"I'll be there then or soon after."

We disconnect, and Kane, now dressed in his pants and nothing else, sits my suitcase that I'd left downstairs on the bed, opening it and pulling out my robe. He motions me forward, and I stand up, slipping my arms into the robe that he's holding open for me before turning to face him. "She thanked me for having you watch over her."

He arches a brow. "Why do I think that's a problem?"

"She was happy that you were watching out for her because you're dangerous Kane, and everyone knows it."

"Everyone doesn't know or that piece of shit wouldn't have played with you last night."

I consider that a moment, setting aside where I was going with this topic for where he's now taken me. "What if he does know? Maybe that makes this more interesting to him."

"Him?"

"Him. Yes. This is a man."

"And you know this how?" he asks, both of us sitting down on the bed.

"Because I know."

"Fair enough," he says, because Kane has done this with me enough times that he knows when that's all he's going to get from me. "So let's say he knows who I am," he adds, "and even thinks, like so many, that they know *what* I am, what does that say about him?"

"I keep thinking that this is the Society keeping me, and through me, you, too busy to focus on them."

"Or?" he presses, because this is what Kane does. He asks me questions; he plays a part in my process in a way that I let no one else.

"Or it could be someone who's followed my career and me. Maybe even someone in law enforcement." I stand up and face Kane, folding my arms and the robe in front of me. "But what if it's not about me? What if it's about Roger? I'm his protégé. They used him to get to me. Maybe this is ultimately about him."

"Why would you go to Roger on this?" he asks. "What don't I know?"

I tell him everything about the call, the cigarettes disappearing, the way Beth was called to the case just as I was. "Damn it! I didn't even find out who called her. I need to know how Beth got there." I grab my phone from the nightstand.

He catches my wrist, standing up and walking me to him. "I missed watching you work."

In that moment, I'm a million pieces of a puzzle that Kane has the power to complete or tear apart. I don't know how to respond besides honestly. "If I let you, Kane, too easily, you will own me and my life again."

"If anyone owns someone, Lilah, it's you owning me."

"No. You will always have secrets. You will always have a world outside of my world."

"Anything you want to know, I'll tell you. Didn't I prove that by telling you how I intend to handle the Society?"

"I missed you, Kane. I missed you more than I never wanted to miss you, but—"

"Don't tell me to walk away, Lilah. I told you. I won't do that again."

"The agency wants to take you down, Kane. *They* believe that you're your father. My job—"

"Murphy knows who I am to you, and he still put you on this task force. Did you ever consider that one of the reasons is me?"

I blink. "What?"

"He knows he can push your limits, and you can push the Society because I'll keep you alive."

My defenses flare. "I keep me alive, Kane. I do."

"We do. *We*, Lilah."

My cellphone rings in my hand, and I glance down at it, but so does Kane, and Lord help me, it's Rich with his shitty timing. Rich, who was just here, trying to get me back and to take down Kane. Kane's jaw clenches. "Get rid of him, or I swear to God, Lilah, I will."

"Because you're not your father, right?"

You don't bait Kane Mendez, and he proves that now. He drags me to him, that lethal quality about him that calls to me far too easily, burning through me. "Get rid of him, Lilah." He releases me and walks out of the bedroom.

CHAPTER THIRTEEN

And the man wonders why I keep pulling my gun on him. I want to grab it and shoot him right now all over again.

My cellphone rings *again*, and I curse, glancing at the caller ID, and of course, it's Rich. *Again.* He's supposed to be in fucking Paris, off the grid. What the hell is going on? The man doesn't learn. He just can't take a hint. I told him to back off, and Murphy promised me that he'd leash Rich. Murphy knew I was protecting Rich from Kane. And Kane's right. Murphy does know who and what he is, and all my suspicions about the many ways that Murphy is more than he seems come back to me.

Rich calls back, and I decline the call. I need to talk to Murphy before I talk to Rich. Right now, I move to the other point my game planning session with Kane brought to light about how Beth got to the scene last night. I dial Beth. "How did you get the call to the scene last night?"

"My supervisor. She just said I was requested by name."

"By who?"

"She didn't say." I can almost see her brow furrow in worry. "Where are you going with this?"

"Find out and call me. And text me your supervisor's name and the exact time of the call."

"*Lilah,*" she presses. "What are you thinking?"

"I'm fact finding right now," I say. "Get me the information. I'll see you soon." I disconnect, and call Murphy who doesn't answer. I call Tic Tac. He doesn't answer. My phone is now ringing; it won't stop fucking ringing, and it won't stop ringing with Rich on the other end. I hit decline and walk to the bathroom, turn on the shower, and contemplate a trip to the Hamptons to grab some more of my things. I'm not going to LA for what I left behind there. I'm done there. I'm here now, and I won't be leaving again. The Society will not get rid of me. I let them run me away once before. Never again.

I step into the shower, and damn it, I flash back to *that* night again, standing under the water, blood pouring off of me, pooling at my feet, and washing into the drain. I have a flash of Kane grabbing my attacker, of me grabbing his knife. I pant out a breath, and suddenly, Kane is there, pulling me close, and I don't even remember him entering the shower.

"They made me a killer," I say. "They have to live with what that means." I shove him against the wall. "And you don't save me. I save me. I don't need your fucking protection, Kane. I don't need you to do my dirty work for me."

He catches me at my neck and turns me into the corner. "Except that I do. The middle, Lilah. We hold onto each other and stay in the middle." He kisses me, and I swear what happens between us in the next few minutes is about how badly I don't want to be in the middle. It's about how badly I want to be just like him. It's about how badly I want to hurt the people who had me raped and killed my mother.

When we're finally out of the shower and I'm dressed in jeans and a T-shirt as well as sneakers, Kane has disappeared somewhere in my apartment while I dry my hair. I glance at my phone to find several text messages. The first from Tic Tac: *See your inbox. Notice that I didn't call for fear you're asleep. I'm setting an example for you on this.*

The next is Beth giving me her supervisor's name and she went one step further. She called her and asked who requested her at the crime scene. The answer: Roger. Of course. I send the info to Tic Tac and ask him the find out who called Beth's supervisor last night. The answer is fast. He already knows. The same number that called Murphy called Beth's supervisor. Umbrella Man was responsible for getting me and Beth to the crime scene. It was assumed but now confirmed.

I start my blow dryer, and turn it off with yet another text.

This one is from Rich: *Damn it, Lilah. You could have picked up. I'm in Europe, and I have to go silent, undercover. You won't hear from me for a while, but I know you made this happen. I know he made this happen, but this isn't over. I'm coming back. I'm coming for you.*

Kane returns and sets a cup of Starbucks coffee next to me on the bathroom sink. He also sets the note I'd received from Junior with my pizza last night next to it. Junior being the crazy person who's been leaving me warning notes since I returned to New York; he's nicknamed for the Stephen King-like mystery and drama that doesn't quite reach King's superior delivery.

I grab the note and read it once again:

M is for Miss me? I missed you.

D is for Disappointed. He's not for you. This city is not for you.

S is for sorry. You are going to be so so so so so so so sorry.

W is for warning. Don't say I didn't warn you.

I set it back down. The "he" is Kane. Junior has made that abundantly clear in the past.

"Obviously Junior isn't going to go away without some encouragement," Kane comments, looking less than pleased, which is about so much more than my safety. Junior's previous notes seem to indicate knowledge of a certain buried body.

"Seems that way," I say. "And like so many people, Junior really hates you. It came with my pizza last night."

"Right before you got called to the crime scene?" he asks, ignoring my snarky remark.

I turn to him. "Yes. Right before I got called to the crime scene." I grab the note, look at it and then him. "You think it's related?" I don't give him time to answer. "It could be related." I glance at him. "If Junior's the Umbrella Man, Kane, you're in danger."

His lips quirk. "We can only hope this asshole comes for me."

"You are not invincible because you're Kane fucking Mendez. You know that, right? You bleed just like everyone else."

"Worried about me, Lilah?"

"Yes. I'm worried about you. There? Are you fucking happy? I'm worried about you. I don't want you to die unless I kill you. That's not a secret." His lips curve into a smile, and I growl under my breath. "You're not listening to me."

My phone buzzes with a text from Beth: *Where are you?*

"I'll give you a ride," Kane says, "and before you resist," he picks up the note and shows it to me, "are you going to do what Junior says and stay away from me? Because that reads like fear to me and fear makes you look like you're weak. It makes you look like prey."

I snatch the letter from him. "You're a manipulative bastard, Kane Mendez." I set the note on the counter and grab my Starbucks coffee, that cup proof of his manipulative skills. "Let's go." I start to pass him and stop. "Rich is in Paris, where he's going dark. He won't be around for you to kill, and at the rate you're going, someone, me most likely, will kill you before he gets the chance to try." Now I walk past him and his low, accented laugh follows.

God, how I both love and hate this man in the very same moment.

We head downstairs and I pull on my rain jacket. Kane steps behind me and helps me settle it around me. I grab my badge that I left in the pocket and turn to face him, holding it in my hand. We stare at each other for several beats. "Put it on, Lilah," he urges.

I put it on.

CHAPTER FOURTEEN

It's all about the blood.

That's what this case is going to come down to. And that's also why I don't comment on Kane's brand spanking new silver 911 Porsche. I don't give a shit what he drives. The truth I won't admit to anyone, even Kane himself, is that I don't really give a shit who he kills or doesn't kill. It's an easy perspective to have while on the way to the morgue; though, there's a reason why I took a nap there last night. Dead people don't bother me. It's the living who get on my last fucking nerve.

Thanks to weather, the traffic is more hellish than usual, and I have time to look through the data Tic Tac sent me, including basics on this new man in Beth's life. There's nothing he's given me that helps me, so I try to call Murphy again. "The bastard and his 'communication is golden' lectures hold no water," I complain when I get his voicemail again. "He's a damn hypocrite. He won't return my calls."

"Murphy doesn't think you communicate well?" Kane asks. "I can't imagine why."

I glance over at him. "I communicate just fine, and fuck you, Kane."

"Exactly my point. You get right to the point."

I shoot him the finger and take matters into my own hands. I dial the one person I know will push the limits. My cousin answers on the first ring. "Lilah, my love."

"Whatever, Lucas. I need to know everything you can tell me about a certain FBI agent. The kind of stuff I'm not supposed to be able to find out."

"What are you going to give me if I do?" he asks, flirting as always.

"What do you want Lucas?" I ask and glance at Kane.

"You," Kane says. "He wants you."

"Oh fuck," Lucas growls. "You couldn't warn me you were with Kane? I'll do the damn search. I'll call you back."

He hangs up, and I laugh. "You cut right past all his bullshit. I take my 'fuck you' back momentarily. He's doing it now."

"I'll bet he is."

"He's my cousin, Kane."

"Your father was his father's stepbrother. He's not your damn cousin, Lilah."

"Okay, well, putting aside all your dirty thoughts—"

"His dirty thoughts."

"Fuck, Kane. Listen to me." I inhale and breathe out. "His father was with my mother when she died. Lucas and I both thought they were having an affair, but Murphy has painted a different picture that involves him. Murphy was in love with her. This entire task force and his hate for the Society are about my mother to him."

"Is it?" he asks, pulling in front of the morgue.

I unhook my belt and turn to face him. "What do you know?"

"There's a window of time where Murphy didn't exist."

"What the hell does that even mean? He didn't exist?"

"I mean he didn't exist, Lilah. Director Murphy isn't who he says he is."

"He works for the agency. Of course, he's who he says he is."

"Or someone with the skills Lucas possesses made him who he is."

"In other words, Murphy changed his identity. Holy fuck." I shake my head. "Holy fuck. Who the hell is he?"

"I'll let you know once I find out."

"Should I have Lucas—"

"No. Don't leave a trail that leads back to you. Let me handle this."

I frown, my mind starting to profile Murphy. Who is he? What is he? That's the thing about Kane; he might be a killer, but he's the killer I know. There's a lot to be said about knowing someone in all their bloody fucked up true colors. There's also something to be said about being with someone who knows all your own bloody fucked up true colors, and still feeling safe.

"You going to kiss me goodbye?"

"Not a chance in hell," I say, but even as I do, I lean over the seat and into Kane. He catches my head and kisses the hell out of me.

"What just happened Lilah?"

"You just fucking happened, and you keep fucking happening. Asshole." And with that, I get out of the car.

The minute I'm outside in the open, I know I'm being watched by some little prick who is either Junior or Umbrella Man or one in the same. I bet this asshole does have a little prick, and he's trying to feel big and important by stalking and hurting women. I want him to come at me. I'll yank his balls right out of his damn pants. I walk in the door of the morgue, eager to get facts and then hole up and start putting all this together. The sooner I get to yank town, the better.

A big Hispanic woman in a security uniform gives me a grimace, which may or may not be because I left a lasting impression. Still on the topic of balls, I asked the kid who was screaming because he thought I was dead last night if he had any to which he proceeded to cry. I asked for an ambulance. I sincerely thought he was having a breakdown. The kid, who is actually twenty-three, needs a new career. He was also the guard in questions *sister*. I didn't know. It's not like I have to try to be an insensitive bitch, I get that, but in this case, I really wasn't being an insensitive bitch.

I make my way to the exam room where Beth and an intern I met last night are already working; both are bundled up in so much plastic that I'm concerned there might be a plague. "Should I be wearing something a bit more formal?" I ask when I enter the room with just my plain clothes on.

Beth pulls down her mask. "I'm cautious with toxins, and you're fine as long as you don't touch anything."

"Like myself or someone else?"

"Oh Jesus, Lilah," Beth says as her intern laughs. I don't know her name, but since she gets my humor when no one else does, I might have to learn it. "The blood from the crime scene," Beth says.

She has my full attention now. "What about it?"

"It was pig's blood."

In other words, we only have two of the three victims the killer claimed when he talked to Murphy. I'm going to assume that number three is either Beth or me.

CHAPTER FIFTEEN

Most people know that I'm not the most sensitive person in the world, but Beth isn't me. She's emotional. She feels shit. I don't know how she stands over dead bodies every day and deals with that kind of baggage, but it's also not my business. I walk to the edge of the exam table. "Let's talk about the toxin that has you all bundled up like it's winter outside."

"You aren't going to say anything about the pig's blood?"

"Don't kill a pig and not make bacon," I say. "The animal gave its life to make that bacon and that's not one of my jokes. An animal's life matters, too, and this time, we don't have to wonder if it's a gateway drug to murder. We already know what he'll do. So, I repeat, what kind of toxin are we dealing with?"

She just stares at me.

"Beth?" I push.

"We don't know," the intern says. "It's none of the known toxins we look for."

"Did we check the pig's blood for toxins?"

"The pig's blood?" Beth asks.

"Yeah. If Umbrella Man had the toxin handy, why not use it on the pig? I mean unless he really did make bacon, but somehow I doubt that."

Beth blinks and then looks at her intern. "Please go ensure that happens."

The intern nods and heads out a side door. Beth motions toward her office. Great. Here we go. Damn it, she's trying to make me a coddler. Kane wouldn't have this problem. She enters her office, and I follow, shutting the door. "I'm being sent to Paris to consult on a case."

Relief washes over me. "That's an experience to embrace."

"Lilah, I know this case. I want this jerk caught."

"I'll catch him."

"I'm not going."

"Yes, Beth. You are. Because if you don't, Kane will have you kidnapped and put in a dark room until this is over."

She pales, and I hate that I just used Kane, but damn it, I need her to listen, and while I'm not someone who leans on Kane, I also prefer to keep people alive. Well, unless I want them dead, but that's another whole part of me for another time and another person.

"Don't do this to me," she says. "Those women were poisoned. I can't figure out how. This is a medical puzzle. I need to solve it the way you need to solve cases, and I would, even if I wasn't convinced I'm a target. I mean, Lilah, we may need special equipment."

"Do they have this equipment in Paris?"

"Yes, it's a state of the art facility, but the bodies are here."

"I'm on this new task force. I'll see if I can keep you involved, but you have to go to Paris. That's non-negotiable. Decide now."

"You can keep me involved?"

"I'm not promising, but I'll try. But if you're dead, I can't do that, now can I?"

She hugs herself and cuts her gaze. "Right." She inhales and looks at me. "Keep me involved. I want to help."

"When do you leave?"

"This afternoon."

"I'm going to have Kane's man take you to the airport."

"Okay."

I pull my phone from my pocket and dial Kane. "Yes, beautiful?"

"Can Jay take Beth to the airport? She's on her way to Paris."

"You think she's safe in Paris?"

"You don't." It's not a question. He thinks the Society is a part of this. I wonder if there will ever be another case where one or both of us won't at least suspect their involvement.

"Why don't I have one of my men go with her?" he suggests, in what is a generous offer.

I glance at Beth, standing there looking like a delicate flower, and I agree. "I'll talk to her."

"Make her listen. Scare the fuck out of her if you have to. You're good at that."

"Thanks," I say, because it's true, and as far as I'm concerned, it's a compliment.

"I tell you you're beautiful, you say fuck you. I tell you you're scary, and you say thank you."

"Your point?"

"We'll discuss my point in person. I'm at my apartment headed to my office here in the city. I'll call my secretary to arrange for a car, and one of my men will be at Beth's disposal. A second car will be waiting on you. Don't shoot the driver. And Lilah, Purgatory still exists, and it's waiting on you." He hangs up.

Purgatory still exists, and it's waiting on me.

Purgatory being what I call my thinking room. He just told me that he kept my room in his apartment here in the city, our apartment at one point. I slide my phone back into my jeans' pocket. "Kane's doing more than providing a ride. He's sending someone to Paris with you. Don't fight it. Just go with it."

"I can't travel with a stranger."

"People travel with bodyguards all the time. They don't know them. They just like knowing they know how to shoot people and kill them. That's where you need to be right now."

"I'll be in Paris. Are you suggesting I'm not safe there either?"

"You can't even tell me how those women died, Beth. You could die. Don't be stupid."

She pales. "You're such a bitch."

"Yeah, I know."

"Are we doing this autopsy or what?"

"You do it. I need to go to the police station and get my hands on the evidence they haven't already fucked up."

"That crime scene was the worst disaster I've ever seen. It was almost like the killer knew Williams and chose her like he chose us."

She's right. That's exactly how this reads. "Call me if you find anything and before you leave for Paris." I turn for the door.

"Lilah."

"Yes?" I ask, glancing over my shoulder at her.

"You and Kane are back together?"

Only a few days ago, I would have quickly rejected that idea. Now, it's not a question I'm ready to answer at all. "Call me, Beth," I say and exit the office.

I walk through the facility, and when I reach the front office, the female guard is no longer there.

A man has replaced her, a tall, broad, stoic-looking man, and I don't like it. I stop in front of him. "Who are you?"

"Clint."

"Clint. Where's the female guard?"

"She quit. I'm her replacement."

"When did she quit?"

"Last week."

Holy fuck. "She was here less than an hour ago."

"If she was here, she wasn't on duty."

"Where were you an hour ago?"

"I took lunch. My lunch coverage was here."

"And that's who?"

"Rick."

"Who was on shift last night?"

"Rick."

"Do you have a picture of Rick?"

"I don't," he replies.

I show him my badge. "I need your supervisor's name and number."

He doesn't so much as blink. "Of course." He reaches in his pocket and hands me a card for Edward Davis. "I'm an ex-Marine, Agent. I assure you I'm here to serve and serve well."

I dial the number, and a man answers. "Ed here. How can I help you?"

"Ed, this is FBI Agent Lilah Love. Tell me about Clint."

"He's an Ex-marine. Highly thought of. What's the problem?"

I eye Clint. "Meet me at the police station, and I'll let you know." I hang up.

Jay walks in the front door. "About damn time," I say. "Is Beth's ride here yet?"

"On the way now."

"Stay here with Clint."

I walk through the facility and back into the exam room to find Beth already working. "You need to leave now."

She pulls her mask down. "Are you fucking kidding me?"

It was just a matter of time. Hang out with me. Become a potty mouth. "Serious as Beethoven at a Jay Z concert. Not as serious as Jay Z at a Beethoven concert. As serious as—"

"Stop. Please stop with the horrible, poorly timed jokes. I get it. You're serious."

CHAPTER SIXTEEN

"Why the sudden urgency?" Beth demands. "Why do I need to leave now?"

"We're on Kane's schedule," I say and then proceed to mumble off some kind of nonsense about traffic and the car she's using to get to the airport. It's a bunch of bullshit that somehow works. Fifteen minutes later, she's updated her paperwork, given me the contact information for the medical examiner who will take over for her on this case, and I've loaded her into the damn car with one of Kane's men.

"Now what?" Jay asks, clearly planning to be my out of the closet shadow.

"Now, you make me believe you're gone again." I proceed to ignore him and the car waiting on me and start walking, not to be an idiot passing up a free ride, but I need to call Tic Tac on the way to the station and do so without an audience, even if that audience works for Kane.

Quickly fading in with the bustle of the Manhattan crowds, I navigate the sidewalks as I punch in Tic Tac's number. "I need stuff."

"You always need stuff."

"I need the security footage for the morgue last night through right now, specifically home in on a Hispanic female guard. I also need information on the security company, the owner, and two additional guards: Clint and Rick. And I need all of this now. The owner is on his way to meet me at the police station."

"What am I looking for?"

"That Hispanic guard quit last week, but she was there last night and today. And wait, shift attention to Detective Williams for about ten seconds. I'm about to be in all kinds of confrontation-ready moments with that wicked excuse of a detective. What do I need to know?"

"She shot and killed a suspect last year that earned her heat with Internal Affairs, including a psych exam. And no, I can't get you the exam."

I hang up on him and call Lucas. "Lilah," he greets. "Should I shout out a hello to Kane as well?"

"You two need to get along."

"Then you two are obviously a thing again."

"I didn't call to talk about Kane."

"You avoid all conversations about Kane. What does that say about you with him, Lilah?"

"That unlike you, I don't like to broadcast my life across all of the Hamptons and beyond. What did you find out for me?"

"I sent you a text. Jess Monroe looks legit. Nothing negative to be found at all. Military service for five years. His father is a Commander. The FBI recruited him, and he's had an exceptional career."

Military service. That takes me back to my conversation with Clint. "What branch of the Military?"

"Marines."

Like Clint. "I'll call you back."

"Lilah—"

I hang up and call Tic Tac. "See if there's a connection between Agent Monroe and Clint the security guard." I arrive at the station. "Text me unless it's big." I disconnect and hurry up the steps and inside the building.

In a few flashes of my badge, I'm at the elevator. I'm about to get on when a familiar rather tall asshole gets off, he's over six feet of asshole in fact. Nelson Moser, a detective I know from recent dealings with him, is most likely connected to the Society. He also worked with my ex-partner Greg, and set him up. And then there's the man he shot and made it look like it was justified.

"Lilah bitch Love," he snaps, his expression as hard as his features.

"If it isn't Dirty Moser," I say. "Oh, I better be nice. You might shoot me in the back and say someone else did it."

He steps closer to my side and says, "Smart girl."

And with that obvious threat he walks away. He needs to be gone. He's *going* to be gone if I get my way, and on this, I will.

I continue on to the third floor, and get busy gathering together the team of staff working these cases, all of whom I consider suspects. It's not long before I have six of the key personnel in a conference room, but there's one important person missing, the lead detective. "Where's Detective Williams?"

Thomas, a thirty-something redhead from the forensics portion of the investigation, explains, "No one can reach her. She's not responding to messages."

There's a short discussion, and everyone agrees: she's missing. "This isn't like her at all," Sally, a gruff, fiftyish woman with wild brown curls declares. "We have a major case launching. She should be here."

This is headed south in a big way fast. "Let's have a unit swing by her house and do a wellness check." One of the girls stands up and volunteers to make it happen.

I wave her onward and then discuss the plan of action with the rest of the team. "What do we know about the victims?" I ask, a pad of paper in front of me, my intent to extract all I can from this team and compare it to what Tic Tac has for me, the likes of which I've only scanned. The group shoots out a recap of basic information:

Victim one: Mia Moore

Age: Twenty-eight

Hair: Blonde, natural

Occupation: Ex-Model turned advertising executive

Parents: Dead

Boyfriend: A rather famous photographer

Siblings: One older brother who is in the Army and overseas right now

Victim two: Shelly Willit

Age: Twenty-eight

Hair: Blonde, bought from a box, which was likely a bad decision on her part, considering Umbrella Man seems to favor blondes

Occupation: Romance novel editor at a major publishing house

Parents: Alive, married, in Texas, both are school teachers

Boyfriend: None

Siblings: None

Hair color, age, city are connected dots. The rest are not but that doesn't matter. This could be about women who snubbed him or women who were nice to him or a great many other ways these women could align for Umbrella Man. I don't miss the fact that he's killing blondes and playing with a brunette.

"Have the families been notified?" I ask.

"Detective Williams handles that," That information comes from Lily, a petite brunette, one of the research girls, *girl* because she reads like a twenty-five-year old teen who needs to grow the fuck up.

"Now you do," I say.

"But—but—"

"You will fight harder to solve the case when it gets personal. Go make it personal."

"Yes, but—"

"Don't finish that fucking sentence. Go now."

She grimaces and hurries out the door. I assign the rest of the team random tasks I need completed when Sally pokes her head in the door. "Detective Williams isn't answering her phone or her door."

I don't even think before I answer. "Tell the officers to go inside her apartment."

Sally pales. "What if she gets mad?"

"She was at a crime scene last night with what I believe to be a serial killer in play and now she's missing. Are you worried about her being mad or dead?"

Sally goes even paler. "I'll have them go into the apartment." She turns away and disappears into the hallway.

I hand out a few more directives and send the team off to do their jobs, all but one that is: I ask Thomas to stay.

"Fingerprints, DNA, what do you have for me?"

"No fingerprint matches in the database. We do have some DNA samples in both victims' apartments. Obviously, we'll need to work on collecting those samples to know what connections to compare. Usually Detective Williams would handle that process."

Of course she would. "Now you do." I don't give him time to tell me that's not his job. It's his fucking job, and I move on. "Talk to me about the cigarettes at the crime scene."

"Cigarettes?" He frowns. "There were no cigarettes in evidence."

"There were fucking cigarettes."

He doesn't even blink before he holds up his hands. "They didn't make it to me."

They didn't make it to him. "Joe Baggley. Do you know him?"

"Yeah, I know Joe."

"I personally handed him one of the evidence bags. Find him. Find it. Put my number in your phone and call me the minute you do." I leave out the part where Detective Williams handled one of the evidence bags herself. She's not blonde, but I have a feeling she's dead or gone, the latter of which comes with a loose meaning, yet to be fully defined.

Thomas stands up and his eyes, blue eyes that are intelligent and cold, in a familiar, straight out of my own looking glass way. He's not something to turn your back on. "She's not coming back, is she?"

"Why do you say that?"

"Because I'm smart enough to see the writing on the wall." He turns and walks out of the room, in what feels like a calculated moment.

If I were anyone but me, he might even stir unease in me, but I'm not, and he doesn't. I wonder if this disappoints him or perhaps thrills him.

Sally rushes back into the room. "She's not in her apartment, but there are no signs of a struggle."

Because the Umbrella Man doesn't do struggles. He's all about power and control.

CHAPTER SEVENTEEN

The officers on scene at Detective Williams' apartment find nothing unusual enough to justify a full legal search, so I'm forced to order them to leave. She could have quit her job because the scene last night was too much for her, especially after her internal investigation last year. She could just be off drunk on booze and chocolate and needing to sleep it off. I even consider the idea that Detective Williams is the Umbrella Man but dismiss the idea. She's not *him*.

That said, the fact that she's gone, added to the fact that evidence has disappeared, leads me to believe the police station is not my best location to work. Well, that and the fact that half of everyone here gives me those blank kind of stares that say no one is home. I swear half of them are doing crack or at least three shots of tequila before arriving to work. I can only hope they're working for the Society. With the case file in my briefcase, I'm ready to leave this hell hole, but I have one more stop: Detective Williams' very personal space.

Entering her office, I pull the door shut and sit down, beginning a search that quickly feels as sterile as Mia Moore's apartment. Everything is in perfect rows, labeled to exactness. There is no dust. There are no doodles on the desk calendar. There is no sign that a human resides here. I consider again the idea that Detective Williams is the Umbrella Man but that idea still won't take root. That said, in this, I do see an OCD-type personality as a potential connection between Williams, Shelly, and Mia, between them and the Umbrella Man, who is calculated in all ways. Could it be a shared boyfriend or family member? I open desk drawers and start my search of Williams' work area, but there's still nothing personal, nothing here that even feels like it's connected to an opinion on anything, not even a menu choice to a favorite restaurant.

I thrum my fingers on the desk, considering what I know about Williams, when an "oh fuck" moment comes to me. This space I'm in right now is owned by the kind of person who would have put on that orange suit and meticulously protected the crime scene. That's not the Williams I met at the crime scene. Was that the real her or is this the real her? Did someone, *did he,* Umbrella Man, or even the Society, for some reason, clean up her workspace? Questions for her staff erupt in my mind, but I also need to know where the hell Ed, the security company owner, is right now, because if he shows up after I leave, another shit show could erupt. I dial the number to his office, and it goes directly to voicemail. I dial the reception desk next. "He's unavailable," a woman tells me. "Can I take a message?"

I hang up.

He's either running or lawyering up. I need to just show up at his office. Grabbing a sheet of paper, I jot down the address for the security company as well as the address for Mia's boyfriend, North Madison. With my destinations in mind, I stand up and head for the door, only to have it open, a big, familiar detective I knew from back in the day now taking up the doorway, a deep scowl on his otherwise handsome face. "Houston, we have a problem," I say, and that's not just a nickname. His actual last name is Houston.

"Yes, we do," he says, motioning me back into the office for what appears to be his request for a private word. "You're in my office."

Considering he's just called this his office, not that of Detective Williams, I find this development interesting enough to do as he says. I give him space and watch him shut the door. "Your office?" I ask.

"I'm the chief now," he says, settling his hands on his hips under his blue jacket, "that makes every office my office," he adds. "And that makes every office, and case, mine."

"You're a young chief," I comment, pretty sure that he's not more than forty. At least that's where my brain wants to place him, and the mildly present lines by his eyes and barely defined nasal folds framing his mouth, seem to confirm.

"I worked hard while you were gone, much, it seems, like you did, *Agent Love*. This isn't an FBI office. Why the hell didn't you come to me before taking over my case?" His voice is now a snap, hard with demand, that wasn't there before now.

"Aside from the fact that your detective ran a shit show of a crime scene, and she's now a no-show to the investigation?" I challenge. "I personally bagged evidence that's now missing."

"What the hell does that mean? It's missing?"

"No one here seems to know it existed, and yet, I handed it off to Detective Williams. I have a responsibility to take control in a case of utter fucking incompetence and multiple deaths."

"I've been in this role cleaning up for six months. You couldn't come to me first and give me a chance to make this right?"

"I had a woman on the ground who'd just died in my arms after I'd been on that shit show of a crime scene, so no. I did what the moment demanded."

"You already used the shit show line. Get a new money line."

I give a fake laugh. "Haha. Aren't you a clever one?" My lips press together. "You want to handle your own staff? Find my missing evidence," I say. I move to pass him and exit the room, but I stop beside him on my way to the door. "And get rid of people like Nelson Moser," I add, Nelson being a dirty detective who I recently linked to the Society. "As long as you have people like him close to you, I will rip your cases from your hands, often and freely." I step forward.

He catches my arm. "Don't make me an enemy, Lilah."

"Hmmm. A subtle threat. I love that shit, especially when you lay hands on me. The main place my mind goes is really delightful. Your gun. My gun. Should we play or are you going to let go of my arm?"

"Fuck, Lilah." He grimaces and lets go of my arm. "That wasn't a threat." He scrubs his jaw and moves, giving me space. "That was frustration. I'm trying to clean up. I'll clean it up."

"Good," I say, handing him my card. "Now you have my number. Text me your number."

"Doing it now," he says, and I watch him type it in and then ping my phone. I have nothing else, so I say nothing else.

I exit the office and then this Godforsaken place, happily, too, the same way I was when I left here the first time. Back when I said goodbye to Roger with a plan to never look back. Suddenly, I wonder if all of this was a plan to get me back in the building, an idea as ridiculous as the one that had Detective Williams as Umbrella Man.

I step out of the station into a cool fall breeze, which feels damn good, because that office was hot and sticky, a miserable affair from start to finish. I pause at the side of the door, focused now on my investigation and where to next. I quickly decide that I want Mia's boyfriend to feel scot-free, even to think that he's not on the murderer radar. That means he needs this worthless crew working for Detective Williams questioning him, not me. On the other hand, I need eyes on him. I believe the same proves true of the security team for the morgue and its owner. There's a connection there. I need to know what it is. I have an office of people at the station who I could have follow these men, but the problem is that I don't trust any of them. I don't trust anyone, but I retract that mental statement quickly.

I trust Kane. I have always trusted Kane. It's me I don't trust. It's him I want to blame for that reality. All of those thoughts bring me to his Fifth Avenue office location. I'm going to ask Kane for another favor. The question is: what will he want in return?

CHAPTER EIGHTEEN

I walk into Mendez Enterprises to find it unchanged from the last time I was here years before, but why wouldn't it be? It's straight up luxury; the way Kane wanted it, the way Kane dictated that it be, and with reason. This is his castle, his creation. He made Mendez Enterprises one of the largest oil companies in the world.

Did he do it with drug money? Maybe.

But he took the money that his father invested, and no matter how much I might press him about his involvement in the cartel, I know this place is his baby. I know he really does pride himself on what he's created. It's why I've always defended him, it's why I always got so damn pissed off at everyone's whispers about his father. It wasn't until *that night* that I hit a wall, and the other side of his two-sided life became an issue for me.

I cross the shiny tile floor of the lobby with a reception desk that matches its gray marble. There are sleek, high-back, brown couches and chairs to my left with an abstract tan rug beneath them and a dozen dangling bulbs above. I step to the front desk and wait for the pretty blonde behind the counter to disconnect a call.

She waves at me excitedly, because Cindy Newman is not only beautiful, she's a sweetheart. She's beautiful that someone else might be concerned she'd have Kane's eye, but I really don't have time to fret over such things, and I'm not insecure that way. If Kane wanted Cindy, he would have Cindy. He just wouldn't have me.

"I can't believe you're finally back," she says when she's free. "Kane told me you might come by."

"Did he now?" I ask. Obviously, Kane isn't insecure either.

"He did. Is this—you know—are you back together?"

"Kane and I are many things. We are," aware of the camera behind the desk that Kane watches a bit obsessively, I look at it, meaning him, and I add, "complicated."

She laughs. "I'm sure he heard that answer, and you definitely made sure he knows you did. You two are something else."

She has no idea. "That we are. Where is he now?"

"In his office. I'd suggest I buzz him, but we both know you're going to go on back. He'd expect nothing less."

Her phone rings, and I round the desk to a foyer that leads to a set of stairs. Kane likes to have a level of stairs between him and any enemy. I know this for a fact. He's told me as much. He doesn't like to have an elevator that could become his prison. His words, not mine. Because, of course, he's his father's son, and even if he were 100% legit, and we both know that's bullshit, he is always a target. He was always his father's son. The death of his mother proves that to be a valid concern. I don't like how valid. I don't think about Kane as vulnerable, but every once in the while, I remember that he's human, even if I don't feel that I am.

I reach the top level of the stairs and turn right to follow a hallway. His secretary here in the city is not at her desk, and I'm again reminded that I know Kane. This is by intent. That man is trying to clear a path and make me feel like I own this office, the way he owns this office. That I belong here and with him. And damn it, it's working. I missed the sense of this place being an escape, even if he wasn't here, because this place was him. I missed all the times I'd come by here and beat up the details of some investigation I was on while he listened, and he did listen.

I don't knock.

I open his door and enter his office to find him standing with his back to me, facing a window that overlooks the city, his expensive gray suit fitted perfectly to his broad shoulders. This place, in all of its professional wonder, fits Kane perfectly, and yet, somehow running a cartel does as well. But the truth is, that air of danger that radiates off of him, that he wears like a second skin, only makes him all the more appealing to me. It always has. On some level, he knows this. I know this. You cannot love Kane Mendez and reject that part of him.

He turns with my entry, his phone to his ear, a glint of surprise in his expression that quickly turns to pure heat and satisfaction. He didn't see me on the camera; he didn't know I was on my way up, but he wanted me to show up here today. And I gave him what he wanted. I don't seem to care either. He speaks to his caller in Spanish, and I pick up enough to know he's dealing with a problem, and he's not pleased.

I shut the door, cross the room and by the time I'm in front of him, he's ended the call. "Problem?" I ask.

His eyes narrow slightly. He's still surprised when I read what no one else does in him. "Nothing I can't handle," he says, but he doesn't reach for me. That tells a story. He's withdrawn, that wall between our worlds present and pissing me off. That wall always pisses me off. It means the cartel is in business, and he's in the cartel's business.

I press my hand to his chest, removing the invisible barrier he's placed between us. "Tell me," I urge softly, my eyes meeting his, and what I find is what I expect: the man who cannot escape being his father's son. "Kane—"

"This isn't one of those things we talk about, Lilah."

"I don't want it to be that way. It's *not* that way."

He arches a brow. "Isn't it, *Agent Love*?"

Anger comes at me hard and fast, and I poke his chest. "Not that long ago, I threw away this badge. You convinced me to put it back on. I guess I know that something changed that night and now you feel like you need that layer of separation. Well, you have it. I should go. You're clearly busy." I try to turn away.

He catches my arm and pulls me to him. "If I told you the cartel killed someone and I'm dealing with the aftermath, then what?"

"*If* you told me? Is this a damn test, Kane? Is that where we're at?"

"*Answer*, Lilah."

"I'd ask what I need to do to protect you and then I'd make it happen. And then I'd beat your ass for being involved at all."

He releases me, his hands settling on his hips under his jacket. "Fuck." He turns away from me and faces the window, tension rolling down his spine. This is a man of control and power, and he's tormented right now.

"Talk to me, Kane," I say stepping to his side.

He scrubs his jaw and faces me. "You know I have a connection that I can't break."

"Family," I say.

"Yes, beautiful, family. I don't want this shit on my doorstep, and I damn sure don't want it on yours, but I was born a Mendez. I will always be a Mendez."

"I know who you are. You can't protect me from that."

"The hell I can't. I am."

"Correction then: you can't protect me from that connection and us do us again."

He catches my arm again, stepping into me, aligning our legs, his voice softening. "Is that what we're doing, Lilah? Doing us?"

"I don't know what we're doing."

His eyes glint hard. "Then I'll handle my own problems." He releases me. "My own way."

"And that means what?"

"You know what that means. You know what I do when things go wrong. I fix things, Lilah."

He's not talking about the cartel. He's talking about burying that body for me. "Fix it with me."

"When you decide you're with me, Lilah, *really* with me, let me know. Until then, I'll fix it on my own." His cellphone rings, and he snakes it from his pocket. "I have to take this."

I stand there and listen, and damn it, he doesn't just speak in Spanish. He speaks in code. I start thinking about the reasons he doesn't like elevators near the office. I start thinking about him being human. He disconnects, and I step to him, my hands on his hips under his jacket. "Who shot who?"

"Lilah—"

"Damn it, Kane. Don't shut me out. People die in your family. Your father was murdered. Has it ever occurred to you that's what rips me to shreds about your damn namesake? Not who or what you are, but that you could die."

"You chase killers, Lilah. Do you think that's easy for me?"

"Don't turn this back on me. Tell me what's going on. Don't make me punch you to find out because I will and—"

He shuts me up by kissing me, and well, literally leaving me panting when he says, "No one gets to kill me but you."

"That's not enough. Talk, Kane."

His jaw tenses. "There's a hit out on my uncle, and if he dies—"

"You inherit the cartel."

"It would be complicated. I need to take care of some things now without you, to protect you." He strokes my hair. "What's happening with Umbrella Man?"

"That's it? *What's happening with Umbrella Man?*"

"Let it go, Lilah."

"No."

"*What happened* with Umbrella Man?"

Damn it, he's shut me out. Cold. Hard. Absolute. I have to let it go because I know him. Pushing now will get me nowhere and I need to focus on the one place I can get results. "Umbrella Man," I repeat, letting him know that I'm conceding and changing topics. "I don't trust anyone in law enforcement for obvious reasons. Can I borrow Jay and a few men to do some surveillance?"

"I'll text you Jay's number, so you have it in your phone. Where do you want him now? I'll get him to come to you."

"I'll handle Jay." I grab his tie. "You just fucking stay alive."

"You're back home, Lilah. I told you. I'm not going anywhere." The air punches with our history and we lean into each other but his damn cellphone rings again.

"Take it," I say flattening my hand on his chest. "Make this problem go away."

He kisses me. "I am. I will." He declines the call and sends a text that pings my phone. "That's Jay's number." Already his phone is ringing again.

I motion for him to take it, and I head for the door. "Lilah," he calls out as I reach for the knob.

I turn to find him holding his hand over the receiver but he doesn't have to ask his question. I know what he wants and I answer before he even speaks. "I'll be in Purgatory." Purgatory—my workspace in his apartment. His eyes heat with this knowledge. "And I *am* back, Kane." With that, I open the door and leave.

CHAPTER NINETEEN

I meet Jay at the coffee shop on the corner, at a table, also in a corner. "Agent Love," he greets, sitting down with me. "I hear I take orders from you now, but your safety comes above all else."

Kane. That fucking man. "His safety comes first. What the hell is going on with him?"

He leans in close. "I'm sure I don't know what you mean."

"You fucking know. Don't make me grab you by your damn hair and yank you over this table."

"He tells you what he wants you to know."

"I'll arrest you."

"He'll kill me," he counters. "I'll take the cuffs."

"Kane won't kill you."

"If you don't believe that man will kill me, you don't know who you're fucking."

"He won't kill you for talking to me," I amend.

"No," he agrees, "but for endangering your life he would, and for involving you in his business endangers your life. Anything you know, you know from him, not me."

"Look, asshole—"

"Call me what you want, Agent Love, but I've seen you work and as such, I know why you two fit. I also know that if anything happens to you, he'll be far worse to answer to than his uncle."

Far worse to answer to than his uncle. It's not exactly what Kane said to me last night, but close enough. That this man sees it, too, tells me what I've always known. Kane is far more dangerous than he's ever allowed me to see. "You keep him grounded," he continues. "And I'm going to keep you alive for all of our sakes."

I lean in closer. "If you get in my way or fuck up my investigation, I'll kill you myself. And I'm no two-trip bitch. I'll get it right the first time."

His lips curve, and he laughs. "You really are a bitch. I heard that about you. I like it. I like you. What do you need from me?"

"Surveillance on a couple of suspects." I talk to him about the boyfriend and the employment offices of both women as well as the entire staff at the security company. "I need this done now, tonight. I'm going to need to get interviews done on these people. I like to watch them squirm a bit before that happens."

"And what keeps Detective Williams from beating you to the punch?"

"She's missing," I say. "I'm working on an electronic trail on her. More on that later. Go. Handle this."

"I go where you go."

"You go where the killer goes."

"It seems to me that's the same thing. You go where he goes." He stands up. "You won't know I'm there and neither will he. Until he's dead." He heads for the door.

He's right. I go where the killer goes but only because the killer leads me there. If that's true, and I believe it is, he'll kill again soon and make sure I'm there for the show. I have to find him first. I consider that a few moments. Will me making a show of hunting for him challenge him or drive him into hiding? I think of all the killers that I've investigated and captured of which there are many. They all wanted attention. They would all do whatever necessary to get that attention. As much as I want to go to Purgatory and think, I need to give Umbrella Man some attention before he demands it by killing someone else.

And so I ask myself: what does he want from me now?

That answer comes easily.

He wants me to look for Detective Williams. I dial Tic Tac. "I've called you three times," he says. "Why is it that you can ignore me, but I can't ignore you?"

"Do you say things like that to Mike? Because if you say that to Mike, you're going to look desperate, and he'll dump you. What does Mike do for a living?"

"All you need to know about Mike is that he isn't rude. He calls me back. You do not."

"I was busy cleaning up pig's blood," I say, though truly I had no idea he'd called me. I was busy with Kane. "Why were you calling?"

"Because I had something important to say."

"Then say it."

"Detective Williams had a juvenile record," he says. "She killed her step-mother."

"And she became a detective," I say. "How the fuck did that happen?"

"Several layers of paperwork, name changes, and a friend of a friend who knew the right people. Sounds like you know who your killer is. This one isn't that complicated."

"Except it's not her."

"It's her," he says. "She's a crazy person."

"It's not her. Send me her address. I'm going over there. And what about family, friends, exes?"

"Her mother's in a nursing home. Her father's dead. No siblings. She does have a boyfriend. His name is Ralph Redman. He's a criminal attorney, and get this, he's got photos of big game he shot hunting. Like a tiger and an elephant."

"He'd know how to slaughter a pig for that blood," I say.

"Wait. You brought up a pig before. You never finished that thought. What pig?"

"I guess you don't know everything. You will, but seriously, you know Williams is missing, and you didn't tell me about the animal killer?"

"What pig, Lilah?" He sounds exasperated.

"Pipe down. There was pig's blood at the first crime scene. Text me the animal killer's address, photo, and anything else I need."

"Done. You have it now. He's in court today. He's representing a stalker. He's that kind of creepy guy."

It could be him, but it still feels off. It's too obvious, like this is what I'm supposed to think, but chasing this lead may entertain Umbrella Man enough to delay another kill. I disconnect the call with Tic Tac and stare down at the photo of a decent looking man with neatly trimmed blonde hair.

My phone beeps with a text from Tic Tac: *I guess we were done?*

I reply with: *I had to kill someone. Currently cleaning up the mess.*

Another text hits my phone, but this one is not from Tic Tac. It's from Roger: *Still waiting on your case file. Did you get mine?*

I stare at the message. I want his file, but I'm not keen on sharing with Roger, not because he's Roger, but rather my concern of corruption within the department. Roger's old school. He's close to the longer termers, and he generally thinks most people are beneath him. I could see him being in the Society.

For now, it's a good excuse to avoid a man I don't want to see. I text him back: *I have yet to sit down to get the file done. Detective Williams is missing. More this evening. I'm walking into an interview.*

I'm about to hit send, but I reconsider. I delete the part about Detective Williams, but I can't say why. My gut just says to keep this quiet. I find Houston's number in the text he'd sent me and hit dial. He doesn't answer so I leave a message.

Roger hasn't replied to my message. That works for me, but his silence won't last. Roger never takes a backseat, and in this case, he's been used by the killer, targeted like I have. If I don't catch this killer quickly, Roger will be here, staring in my eyes and judging me.

I stand up to leave and it's as if the man heard me, my phone buzzes with a text, and damn it, it's Roger: *We got our man here. I'm coming back.*

I want to throw up. I set my phone down but manage to stare at his message. He's coming back. Fuck. Fuck. Fuck. Inhaling, I reach in my field bag and pull out a photo of me and Kane, flipping it over to the marks I've made there. A mark for every murder I've solved since *that night*. That's what Roger will see, the profiler who's caught hundreds of killers. Not the profiler who is a killer. Not the profiler who killed easily. Not the killer who knows she could do it again.

The only person who sees that part of me is Kane. And he's the only one who will ever see her.

CHAPTER TWENTY

I catch an Uber to the apartment of Detective Williams' boyfriend.

If I were anyone else, I might call Kane during my ride just to have him tell me I'm right; no one but him knows me or sees the real me. But I know this to be true. I don't need a fucking man to tell me so. And I hate whiney, needy people who need to be coddled. I'm not going to become one of those people. Luckily, right as I'm about to call him anyway, my brother calls, and there is really nothing better in this world than a sibling punching bag.

We get that party started right out of the gate. "You coming home for the weekend or staying up there with your criminal boyfriend?" he asks.

"Says the guy dating his ex and taking hand me downs."

"Oh fuck, Lilah. Did you really go there?"

"Since you're dating that bitch, yes."

"Speaking of being a bitch, *Lilah*."

"Did you call just to tell me you love me or what?"

"I called because dad's holding a fundraiser Friday night. You said you were going to be supportive. He's running for Governor of our great state, sis. That's big."

"I know, but—"

"Already the but—"

"I've got a problem here," I say, abbreviating to ensure the driver doesn't put two and two together, but he doesn't seem to know much English anyway. "And," I add, "that problem's hyper-focused on me. I'm not bringing him to you."

"What the hell does that mean? A killer?"

"Yes."

"Hyper-focused on you? What the fuck Lilah?"

"You need to relax. This is what I do, Andrew. And I'm in an Uber, so don't ask for details. I'm fine."

"How safe is your apartment?"

"Kane basically hired me a bodyguard, and I'm going to stay with him tonight."

"Thank god for your criminal boyfriend."

"Hanging up, Andrew." And I do.

He calls back. "The fundraiser is at the Metropolitan Museum in the city. Show up. Bring Kane. Tell him to donate big."

"I can't. Not with this situation."

"There will always be a situation. That's who you are. I'm calling Kane to invite him."

"Don't call—" He hangs up and I murmur, "Kane."

I dial Kane. He answers on the first ring. "You okay?" he asks.

"Am I okay? Why are you answering like that, asking me if I'm okay? You do know who I am, right?"

He laughs. "Yes, Lilah. I know very well who you are. Please forgive me for asking if you're okay."

"My brother—"

"Is calling me right now."

"Yeah, don't answer. It's an invitation to a fundraiser for my father that we aren't going to." The Uber stops in front of Ralph Redman's apartment building, and I get out. "That's all I had to say. You go take care of your assholes. I'm presently working on mine."

I watch a man walk toward the door that requires a code which means he's my way in the building. "I have to go." I hang up and rush after him, catching the door before it closes, and enter. I step into the entryway, and it's reminiscent of Mia Moore's place. Small foyer. Mailboxes to the left. Stairs directly in front of me. It's not fancy, but it's an expensive city to live in. My phone buzzes with a text, and I grab my phone to find a message from Kane: *I accepted your brother's invitation. We can fight about it in bed tonight.*

I scowl and shove my phone back into my field bag. He probably didn't even accept. He's just trying to piss me off. He enjoys pissing me off. I'll deal with him later. For now, I start up the stairs, stopping at level two. There are four door options, two right and two left. I go left per the address indicated. I'm a few steps further down the hallway when I realize that Redman's door is open. I grab my weapon and then my phone, dialing Tic Tac. "Don't ask questions," I say when he answers. "Is Redman in court right now?"

"Checking."

I can hear him punching the keyboard before he says, "Yes. He's in session now."

I disconnect and shove my phone in my waistband, approaching the door and kicking it open. "I'm behind you," Jay calls out.

I hold my hand out behind me, telling him to back off. I enter the apartment, scan the small living room, and find nothing. Jay steps to my side and I trust him because Kane trusts him. No, Kane trusts no one. I trust him because he's afraid of Kane, which is a thought I'll need to be uncomfortable with later when I have more time. I motion Jay right, down a hallway. I go left. I've just cleared a small workout area when I hear, "Holy fuck."

I hurry back down the hallway toward his voice, joining him in a bedroom where I find a dead pig with a bullet hole. It was shot to death. The absence of blood on the bed tells me it didn't happen here. "How the hell did he get it up those stairs?" Jay asks. "And why?"

My cellphone rings, and when I find Tic Tac's number, I answer. "Yes, Tic Tac?"

"Ralph Redman just shot and killed himself in the courthouse. He's dead."

I hang up. Most people will now believe that Ralph was the killer, but that's a bunch of crap. The real message is one of control. The killer controlled Ralph. He made him kill himself, and like the pig, he was shot because he was inconsequential to the killer.

CHAPTER TWENTY-ONE

"What kind of wicked fuckery is this?" Jay asks from beside me. "Is the cartel involved? Fuck. I need to call Kane."

"No." I holster my weapon. "This isn't the cartel. It's just my job. Sick bastards are what I do, and Kane doesn't need a phone call every time I deal with one of them."

"In this case, he needs a call."

"Holy fuck," I say, grabbing my phone and dialing Kane myself.

"Lilah."

"If your man can't handle the sick fucks I deal with all day long, he needs to not be your man with me."

"You really are a bitch," Jay bites out.

Kane laughs. "What sick fuck scared Jay?"

"The one who put a dead pig in a bed. I'm hanging up now."

"Lilah," Kane says, and there's expectation in his voice. He knows I don't usually call him at all, let alone incessantly.

"Yes, Kane?"

"Glad you finally accepted protection."

"Fuck you, Kane Mendez." I pull my gun and point it at Jay. "Should I kill him now?" Jay curses as I add, "Will that be enough acceptance for you?"

"He's a good guy, Lilah. Don't kill that one." He hangs up.

I grimace and lower my weapon. "He told me not to kill you, but I don't follow Kane's orders."

"I'm not your enemy, Lilah, but whoever put that pig in the bed is. Now what?"

"I was trying to figure that out when you distracted me with Kane fucking Mendez." I point at him. "Stop talking." I turn away from him and consider how any move I make creates another move by the killer. If I call him on this, if I tell the world he did this, not Redman, all I do is become a worthy opponent. I need him to believe that I'm stupid enough to believe he's dead.

I dial Houston, and he picks up right away. "Agent Love."

"Oh you answer your phone now but don't return calls?"

"I was taking care of a problem for you. And I was about to call you back. You'll be happy to hear that Moser is on leave and under investigation."

"Good," I say. "Fine, whatever. What about—"

"That's all I get?"

"Yes. What about—"

"The missing evidence hasn't shown up. I talked to Joe. He said Williams took it from him. She's still missing. I'm working on a search warrant to properly search her apartment. I should have it by morning."

"I'm about to make your search warrant easier. Detective Williams' boyfriend has a dead pig in his bed, which I suspect is the pig that matches the blood at the Mia Moore crime scene. Additionally, if you haven't heard, he just killed himself in an open courtroom."

"Holy hell. That was him? And you know this before me how?"

"Because I'm doing my job."

"And I'm not?"

"I'm texting you the address. Get me a forensic team here, and I'll meet the team at Detective Williams' place when you get the warrant. No one goes in without me. And see if we have camera footage somewhere. This bastard got a large pig in the building. Someone had to see that."

"Is he our guy?"

I hesitate. I want to tell him no, but I don't know who's dirty and who's not. I don't know who is Society with some fucked up agenda I don't know about or understand. "Just get me my team over here. And find my fucking evidence." I hang up on him and turn to Jay. "You need to leave. You'll have to be interviewed officially if you stay."

He nods and heads for the door. "Jay."

He turns to face me. "You didn't save my life or anything, but you tried twice now. I won't kill you. I might even save you if it's in reverse."

He laughs. "You're welcome, Lilah." He exits the bedroom.

"Yeah, thanks. Whatever." I turn back around and stare at the poor pig, and my gut twists. I like animals more than most people. They don't have attitudes and agendas. They aren't inconsequential at all. They're the necessary pure good in a world of evil. It's hard to protect asshole humans, some of whom I'd rather kill my damn self at times. Protecting animals feels like a part of how I repent, how I make up for being one of those asshole humans. The thing about humans who are scared, who know they're about to die, is that they become animals and this asshole knows it. I realize that now. He clearly believes animals to be inconsequential. He clearly made sure those women, and Redman, felt inconsequential before they died. That's his message. I get it. I understand it and him.

What he doesn't understand about me is that when he killed the pig, he made sure I wouldn't arrest him. I'm going to kill him. And I'm not going to feel bad about enjoying this one.

LISA RENEE JONES

CHAPTER TWENTY-TWO

It's my expert profiler opinion that Umbrella Man has a sparkling clean toilet. Redman does not.

I don't wait on the forensic team. I start searching Detective Williams' boyfriend's apartment and what I find is a big fat nothing. That's actually not true. He's a slob. I stand at his nasty ass bathroom toilet that hasn't been cleaned in what I estimate to be six months and grimace. I've decided I don't like buckets of blood and dead people's toilets, at least not Redman's. It's truly disgusting, and it's also not Umbrella Man's. Umbrella Man is anal. He's precise. He's a guy who cleans his bathroom. He's not the guy who has shit hanging around on their toilet seat. And where does this lead me? Besides a memory of a Mr. Clean commercial? Redman is so far from "the guy" that I'm not sure Umbrella Man would believe it if I said this was the guy. It's tempting to buy time to hunt Umbrella Man and say that he is, but I don't believe Umbrella Man to be that stupid. He didn't pick me because I'm stupid. He's playing a game. I need to make sure that game becomes mine. I can't do that when I haven't even sat down and analyzed the case properly.

I need to be in Purgatory, away from this sick fuck long enough to figure out the sick fuck.

For now, I'm stuck in this hellhole with a dirty toilet that I know isn't going to tell me shit unless Umbrella Man wants me to know. It's that thought that drives me forward, looking for another message. By the time the forensic team arrives, I haven't found any other significant find. The dirty toilet and the pig pretty much sums it all up. That pig deserves justice. I can't say what Redman deserves. I didn't know him. All I know is that he was a filthy bastard who didn't kill himself. He did it for a reason, and there's really only a few ways you can convince someone to kill themselves: shame, fear for someone else, or a dreadful future, which could mean prison, but it could also mean loss of limbs, eyes, or the tool between his legs. Yes, I'm a sick fuck, too. That's how I catch sick fucks. I go where someone a little less sick won't. Williams is missing. Redman was dating her. Maybe killing himself was about a choice Umbrella Man gave him. He had to choose himself or her. It's a thought worth exploring.

It's near four when the search warrant clears for Detective Williams' apartment. I meet the team there, and because this is my crime scene, they damn sure cover their feet and hands. While they get wrapped up and covered, I'm the first in the door and alone by choice. I do a quick walkthrough to confirm what I already suspected: Detective Williams isn't here, not even in pieces.

Houston arrives shortly after I've allowed the team to enter the property with Thomas, the team forensic expert I'd met at the station. "This feels awkward," Thomas says when I meet them at the front door. "She's my damn boss."

"I'm your fucking boss," I say. "Suck it up and get in there and find something you wouldn't find because you know her."

Houston motions him forward. "She's right. Do your fucking job."

Thomas sighs and heads into the apartment. Houston motions me into the hallway. "Anything?" he asks.

"If you mean is Williams here? No, she's not. I have no idea where she is, but I could have told you she wouldn't be here before we ever arrived. She wasn't here when we looked for her before."

"What do you know that I don't know?"

"Aside from the fact that she wasn't here when we were here before, and that he isn't dumb enough to show up at a place that's on our radar?"

"*He*? Like I said. What don't I know?"

"Nothing I feel like sharing, considering you can't keep up with evidence," I reply.

"If the lead detective was dirty, Agent fucking Love, what do you expect from me?"

"I expect your whole department to be investigated."

"It was, which is how I got this job. I'm cleaning up, which is exactly why acting on Moser was so damn easy for me. I don't like the bastard, I don't trust the bastard. I'm not the bad guy here. Ask Murphy. I called him. He told me to tell you to call him."

"Name dropping irritates the fuck out of me," I snap.

"Being judged unfairly irritates the fuck out of me," he replies, "especially when it's not deserved. *Call* Murphy. I was put here for a reason, Lilah Love."

Houston could be leading me into a trap, baiting me to find out what Murphy wants by placing me here in New York City, which is why I answer him with as direct of a fucking answer as possible. I turn away and enter the apartment again, leaving him in the hallway.

This time, I look at the room with new eyes, and the first thing I focus on is the desk in the corner. I walk over to it and do a visual scan. The top is clear, clean, freshly polished. I open the center drawer. It's nearly empty with a few neatly placed pencils and a notepad inside. I move to the side drawer and pull it out. The files inside are neatly lined up and labeled. I kneel and look through them to find basic categories like taxes, warranties, and receipts, all of which seem to be what she says they are. She uses H&R Block, and she did her taxes late and recently. I take a picture of the accountant's information who worked with her, as well as the receipts that might lead me somewhere, though none of this feels relevant. There is a birthday card, too, from "your sister forever." She doesn't have a sister. I shoot a photo of the return address and send it to Tic Tac with a message: *find out who this person is to Williams.*

I scan the room again and come to a bottom line: the anal nature of the files fits the setup that I found at the station in her office. It fits what I know of the killer. I have to consider that she might be the killer, but my gut still tells me that's not the case. I stand up and shut the drawer, turning to move on when I all but run into Thomas, who is actually quite big and tall. And while his stance might seem unassuming and accidental, that's bullshit.

"Personal space. What the hell?"

He stares at me for a few beats. "I didn't expect you to run into me."

"And yet you walked up behind me?"

"It's a small space."

"So is the place between your legs where I'll put my knee if you don't take a step out of my personal space."

His eyes narrow, and he steps back. I step forward right back into his space. "Next time I'm this close to you, you'll feel it for all the wrong reasons. Did you need something?"

He doesn't back away. Neither do I. "To make a general comment."

"Which is what?" I ask.

"She didn't strike me as being as neat as this apartment. Her sheets are perfect. Her towels are perfect. Her drawers are perfect."

"And yet?" I prod.

"Her hair was usually a mess. She spilled her coffee often. Something was usually hanging out of her purse."

And he noticed. Why did he notice? Innocent observation? Maybe, but I don't think so. "What's your relationship with Detective Williams?"

"I observe people. That's all."

"And what did you observe?"

"I told you. She's not this organized. It feels off. So off that I felt like she wasn't fit to oversee the investigation."

"What else?"

"I saw her get frazzled a few times during the past month after taking a call. She'd go into her office and shut the door."

"Was that abnormal?"

"I didn't work with her directly before this case," he says.

"And yet you mentioned it."

"Yeah," he says. "What about it?"

"Would it surprise you to hear that her office is just as organized as her apartment?"

"It just doesn't fit what I saw when she was in front of me, but hell, maybe she's a contradiction or maybe she overcompensates for one thing with another."

Or maybe, I think to myself, *she didn't organize any of this herself.* Maybe it's all the Umbrella Man. It's a crazy thought but then crazy is what I do.

"Gather evidence," I order. "Let me know what you find." But he won't find any. Because the Umbrella Man doesn't want us to find anything. This entire scene is staged.

I think about every crime scene involved in this case and find myself questioning if all of the girls were actually scattered and disorganized until Umbrella Man arrived. What if the he cleaned them up or even made them clean up? I can almost picture them all cleaning desperately to stay alive. Would it have happened during a kidnapping before the murder? Every part of me wants to leave this apartment and do what I have to do to follow my thought process right now, but I blink and find Thomas staring at me, something in his eyes I don't like.

"Go work," I order.

"Yes, ma'am, Agent Love." He turns away from me, and I swear I heard a hint of a laugh in his voice.

CHAPTER TWENTY-THREE

Where is Detective Williams?

It's the question of the day. It's the question Chief Houston asks when he catches me at the front of the apartment before I leave. "If not here, where?" he asks.

"I don't know."

"You're the profiler. If she's dead, where is she now?"

"If she was dead—" I stop myself short, because unlike a lot of irritating people on this case, I don't have foot to mouth disease. "We don't know if she's dead."

He studies me hard and heavily. "Tell me where your head is right now. What the hell can I possibly do to help you catch this asshole if I don't know what rabbit hole we've fallen inside?"

"I like to travel my rabbit holes alone rather than with a wolf that might eat me."

"You're no rabbit, Lilah," he snaps, folding his arms in front of his chest. He's big like Thomas, but he stays the hell in his own personal space. I still don't trust him. "You still don't trust me," he comments, like he heard what I thought. Hell, maybe I said it out loud.

"Nope," I say, sticking to the less is more idea.

"Okay then. At least you're honest. I'm assigning Detective Carpenter to take over as lead for Williams, reporting to you, of course. You know him. You worked with him. He knows Williams."

He's right. I know him. I've worked with him. He's an old geezer with a bald head. "Knowing him doesn't mean I trust him. It doesn't even mean I like him."

"He knows Williams."

"You said that."

"You don't. He can offer insight into where she might be right now."

"Fine. Have him call me." I turn to walk away.

"Agent Love."

I grimace and pause, turning on my heels. "Yes?" I ask.

"Who can I give you that you *will* trust? Who do you want on this case?"

"Greg," I say of my old partner. "He's on leave because Moser set him up to take the fall for something he didn't do. Payback because Greg knew he was dirty and wasn't going to put up with it."

"If I get him back?"

"Get him back. We'll talk a bit more if you get that done."

"You're riding me like I'm a drunk fool, Lilah."

"Agent Love to you, asshole, until you prove you're not a drunk fool."

"Call fucking Murphy and the 'fuck' in that sentence is me trying to relate to you because nothing else is working."

Umbrella Man has a better chance of relating to me, but that's my little secret. "Did you want a cookie or a proper lesson on pronunciation? Because you need to emphasize the F or the K in appropriate moments."

He doesn't laugh. "I'll get your man back." He presses his hands to his hips. "We have an issue though. The press got hold of all of this. They're breathing down my neck. What am I giving them?"

"You have a suicide in a courtroom. Leave it at that."

"I have two dead women. They know."

"That, to the public eye, don't connect."

"The attorney general wants this case solved before panic sets in," he counters.

"And let me guess, you told him that Ralph Redman is our killer?"

"Someone told him. It wasn't me. And he has a reporter threatening him with a serial killer headline."

Someone told him. The Umbrella Man told him. Killers want attention. He wants my attention, and he wants pressure on me to give it to him. Somehow, someway that bastard relayed the message to the press that he wanted to get out to the public.

"Give him what he wants," I say, and I'm not talking about the attorney general, though I'm certain that's what Houston will think. I'm talking about Umbrella Man. He wants it. Let him think he gets what he wants. For now. Until I get him.

I turn away and skip the Uber, despite the long walk ahead of me to Kane's apartment, considering the sensitive calls I need to engage. I try Tic Tac and get his voicemail. I dart into a Starbucks where I order a mocha with a triple shot. My agenda with that caffeine high is to make myself a little less approachable than everyone has seemed to find me the last twenty-four hours. I've just exited to the street again when my cellphone rings with my returned call from Tic Tac.

"I need—" I begin.

"You always do," Tic Tac replies. "First, before I forget, the sister you asked about is a sorority sister."

I check that question off the list. "What else?"

"Ralph Redman. I assume he's your killer?"

"If only it were that simple, but this is far more evil than a man who did his dirty work and offed himself when he was done. Consider Redman a victim."

"He killed himself."

"Like I said, consider Redman a victim. And somehow, someway, all of these cases connect to someone in law enforcement. There's no other conclusion when we have someone calling themselves Roger getting to key supervisors and evidence missing. Look at everyone connected to me or Williams for the past year."

"What the hell is this? Redman killed himself."

"Okay, Tic Tac, let me be clear. If someone was holding a gun to Mike's head and told you to shoot yourself or they'd shoot him, what would you do?"

"I guess it comes down to if I actually believe the person holding the gun really will shoot."

"You believe him. What do you do?"

"Shoot myself," he says. "That's Evil."

"The kind you don't underestimate. The kind Stephen King makes up in his books and is never real, except it is." I don't give him time to reply. I need stuff. Now. "I need you to do an interview for me."

"Me? I don't do interviews. I'm the tech guy."

"I can't trust anyone. I trust you. I need you to make calls yourself. Find out from the family and friends of Mia and Shelly if they had OCD. Find out from medical records. Find anyone close to them who are."

"Where is this headed?"

"Just find out. I need to make another call."

"Lilah—"

"Jeff," I say, making this personal. "He's going to kill again. Most likely Detective Williams, who I predict to be a prisoner right now. Make the calls. Make them quickly. And get me a timeline for the victims. Did they disappear before they were killed? When were they last seen? Who last saw them?"

"Has the local law enforcement found out nothing?"

"I had evidence disappear that I personally bagged on scene. So, have they found out anything? I have an entire file they put together, but I trust nothing I'm told by them. Am I going to tell you what it says, no. I want what we do to be untainted by what they do."

"Aren't people going to be irritated that I call again, after they already heard from the police?"

"And you know what you say to them if they do? You say, so sorry to irritate you with a murder. Did the victim irritate you as much when she was alive? That'll shut them up." There's a tingling sensation down my spine. I'm being watched. "If you need help, call Murphy. I need to go."

I hang up and pause at a corner by a light, discreetly scanning the area. "Are you here?"

"Yeah."

"So is he. I feel him."

"You want to try and trap him?"

"If only he were that stupid. He doesn't know you're there. Make sure he doesn't. I'm going to Kane's."

"I figured that out, and I think that's smart."

"Well, that's exactly what I needed: your opinion. Because if you didn't think it was smart—"

"This part of you is inbred, isn't it?"

"My really funny jokes? Yes." I move on. "Kill him if you see him. I'll take the blame. You have my word."

"I don't need to be told twice."

I disconnect and dial my old partner, Greg. The light changes as I leave him a voicemail. "I got your job back on a big case. Call me. Now."

I disconnect and dial Kane. "Lilah."

"Watch your back. This asshole wants me. He could come at you."

"Where are you?"

"On my way to Purgatory."

He's silent a moment, digesting the fact that I'm really going to go to his place. "I have some business to finish up, but I'll be there soon."

"Good. Someone has to protect you."

"But who's going to protect you from me, Lilah? Isn't that always your question?"

"I do believe I've proven myself quite capable where you're concerned, Kane Mendez. You can test me tonight, if you so please."

He laughs, low and deep, and disconnects. Fuck. I love that man's laugh. If Umbrella Man comes for him, he'll be sorry, because if he touches Kane, I'll stop pretending I don't like killing assholes like him. I'll embrace my inner Dexter. Who am I kidding? If Umbrella Man goes at Kane, Umbrella Man will end up in a corner sucking his thumb, suffering until Kane hands him to me in pieces.

What does it say about me that I know this about Kane and still Kane remains the only person in my life who knows and understands me?

CHAPTER TWENTY-FOUR

I walk into the Madison Avenue building where Kane lives, where we both used to live, and I swear to myself I'm not going to make a big deal out of being here. It's not a big deal. I need to use Purgatory. I'm not moving back in. I'm not getting that serious with Kane again, but even as I have that thought and step onto the stone floors of the lobby, memories crash over me, impossible to escape. So is the security desk to the right of the door, where the security guard, Kit—a tall, brooding, fit Mexican man who smiles big and kills easily—greets me. I like him, and it's not for his smile.

"Lilah fucking Love," he greets. "I heard you were back."

"I'm certain that wasn't Kane, considering he wouldn't presume that I'm back just because I'm in the same city."

He laughs. "No comment." He winks. "Glad to have you in the building." He sets a long yellow envelope on the counter. "This came for you."

I take it and glance at him. "From who?"

His attention sharpens. "A courier delivered it. Problem?"

"I'll let you know after I look at it." I lower my voice. "I have an enemy. A dangerous enemy. The kind that might scare someone like say you, and with good reason."

"Kane informed me of the situation. I've taken precautions."

"Even when you're not here?"

He arches a brow but doesn't ask a question. "Yes," is all he says. But then, this is Kane's man, after all. He's seen far more than I can probably imagine.

"Okay then. Power on." I don't wait for agreement, I start walking, but I don't even think about opening the envelope here in the middle of the lobby. Without hesitation, I punch in a code in the elevator, certain it will work. The car moves and carries me to the seventeenth floor. The doors open, and I step into a small foyer that's nothing more than stone floors and glass walls to allow Kane to see who has entered. The panel next to a silver door that lifts requires fingerprint entry—that's how careful Kane is— and that's how present I still am in this apartment. I walk to the panel, stick my finger on the pad, and the sliding silver doors before me open.

Kane will now be notified of my presence.

I enter the apartment, and I try not to let the room affect me. I see it, I do, but it's just a room of towering ceilings and windows, with gray wooden floors. There above, connected by three levels of glass and tiled stairs to my left, are just rooms. It's all beautiful. It's stunning. It's dripping with money, but none of this defines me or Kane. Blood defines us. Murder defines us. I can't forget how we came to be and how we divided.

I walk to the main living area distinguished by a gray rug and a distinct accent wall, with a massive painting of the cove where we used to go to talk. He had that painting custom made when I moved into this place with him. I sit down on one of the light gray chairs, accenting the gray couch and coffee table, and focus on the envelope.

I set it on the coffee table and slide my bag onto the couch, pulling out a pair of gloves, before I open it and find a file with a note on top:

Agent Love:

Houston is with us. His file is included for your review. We align. Trust him. Your friend, Greg, I vetoed his involvement. He is not what he seems. Call me after you read the file.

—Murphy

Irritated, I grab my phone and call him now. "How do you know where I'm at? Are you having me followed?"

"Agent Love, I don't have to have you followed to know that you'll be with Kane Mendez."

"Kane and I—" I hesitate. "Did you give me this job because of Kane?"

"You are what matters, but yes, you're a complete package, and yes, Kane is part of that package. Does that bother you?"

"Kane is a complicated man."

"Kane is a powerful man who frankly scares the shit out of me, Agent Love, but I don't run from what scares me. If I did, I'd run from you. What do I need to know about today?"

"That's it. You'd run from me and Kane? Because you don't seem to get it. Kane will kill you."

"And you wouldn't?"

"Are you going to give me a reason?"

"That certainly isn't the plan. Back to today."

"Today was a test. Today was staged. No one but me and Tic Tac knows that."

"I'll trust your reasoning on that, but I hope that you choose to tell Houston. I won't. Read his file. And stay safe, Agent Love. I have big plans for you." He disconnects.

I toss my phone down and pull off the gloves, tossing them on the table next to it. I intend to look at Houston's file, but Murphy's words come back to me: *Kane is a powerful man who frankly scares the shit out of me.* My gaze goes to that painting of the cove, memories rushing back at me. It was there, with nothing but the ocean to hear us, that Kane first told me who and what the Mendez name meant, what rumors had already told me. It was there that he told me about killing a man who planned to kill him for being his father's son. It was there that he confessed so much to me. It was there when I'd told him about my first kill. No. Not my first kill. It was there that I told him about the first time I could have cuffed and arrested, but I pulled the trigger on the monster instead. He'd raped a little girl and he'd dared me to shoot him, and I just—I did. It was wrong, but it felt necessary. And Kane's reply had been: *Next time, let me do it for you.* And he'd meant it, even if, at least back then, I'd told myself he didn't.

But he had meant it. He'd kill for me. He wouldn't even ask why. He'd just do it and feel no regret. It's what he learned. It's how he survived, in ways no one but me and the cove will ever know. Because that cove holds many a secret we told each other. I could destroy Kane. But he could destroy me, too. What concerns me isn't Kane. It's the way Murphy seems to understand us. It feels like he knows more than he should, but then Kane said there's more to Murphy than I know. Is there a history between them that Kane hasn't told me?

CHAPTER TWENTY-FIVE

That question about Kane and Murphy will be answered by Kane, right here in this very apartment.

With that decision made, I set my concern aside and head down a hallway and into the kitchen, which is, of course, big and glorious, with a giant gray stone island fit for an Iron Chef who is not me or Kane. He has, however, hired a chef to cook for us a few times, and I enjoyed every minute of that eating. The rest of the time, I microwave with excessive skill, even Kane agrees.

Spying the fancy coffee pot on the corner of the counter, I head in that direction and grab the canister next to it and inhale. Oh God. He has the French bean I adore so much. God, I've missed this stuff. I start a pot and open the fridge to find a big container of strawberries, which Kane knows I love. The man buried a body for me, and he even buys me strawberries. It's hard not to see that devotion as just a little appealing. I open the freezer and there is Haagen-Dazs strawberry ice cream. I grab it. "My God, I think I'm I love with this man again." Those words are out before I can stop them, and I set the ice cream on the island.

"Okay, Kane," I call out to his many recording devices, "if you're listening or watching me right now, which I'm sure you are because that's the kind of sick fuck you are, I didn't mean that literally. I'm not sure where we are right now. I might still hate you. I do still hate you." I open a drawer and pull out a spoon. "The coffee and ice cream are pretty nice touches, though, I do have to admit, but you always did do that Latin, smooth operator stuff. I know how you are. I know *who* you are, and it's not all strawberries and ice cream." I grimace. "And Jesus, I'm talking to a camera like it's fucking Kane."

I set my ice cream and spoon aside and walk to the coffee pot, starting my brew, and with my ice cream melting and my coffee percolating, I head back to the living room, grab my bag and the file and head upstairs to the third level, which is Kane's bedroom. I step inside, and I don't even think about stopping to look at that massive gray-framed bed. I know he records this room. He won't be watching me stare at the bed we used to fuck in. Often. We did that often. I miss that, too, but I get a lot more work done when I'm not always distracted by being naked with Kane Mendez.

Therefore, I can't move back in here; I won't. It doesn't matter that Murphy already thinks I have. This is far more complex than what Murphy wants. I walk right past that very big, very comfortable bed and head straight to the door on the far wall, entering the room that Kane built for me— my Purgatory, the place that I exile myself until I solve a case. He wanted it here, so I'd be closer to him. I scan the perfect version of the same room I have setup at the beach house. It's round, the walls covered in a film-like material that I can write on. There are pushpins and moveable boards in various places. Of course, there's a desk and a chair, but there are also two more chairs and a wall of the best forensics books in existence that Kane gifted me. Books that I read when I either had a brain freeze, I'd never admit to anyone, or I just needed inspiration. Kane reads them too. I try not to think about that being inspiration for him, too.

I sit down at the desk, and there is a brand-new MacBook waiting for me. I know it's brand new because the box is sitting beside it. Opening the lid, I find a screensaver of our painting downstairs, and I instantly know the password, as Kane knew that I would: The Cove.

Ready to analyze all my case data, something long past due, I head back downstairs to arm myself with my snacks. Once there, I fill a huge insulated mug with coffee, punish it with cream and sugar, in a way that would make Kane cringe, before snapping up my ice cream. Soon, I'm behind my desk, keying up my email and sipping my coffee, while my ice cream softens even further. I don't want to have to work for it when I eat it. In fact, I'll drink it over fighting it like it's a concrete block. I do enough fighting without fighting my ice cream, too.

Soon, I'm staring at my inbox, which is my business email, merged with my personal email, and apparently, Viagra can make all my troubles go away. It certainly gives you a lift. If only Umbrella Man would have gotten this email and tried it. I scan through all the junk and find the messages from Tic Tac and Roger. Roger's subject line references his now closed case. I'm not sure I can write off anything to do with Roger, considering he was used to get me to the scene of the first known murder, but for now, it's right to the back burner for him. With that decision, I begin going through Tic Tac's notes, even printing them out. There's a stack of notecards on the desk, and it's time to do my thing. I need a card for every person involved in this case. I start with victims:

Mia Moore

Shelly Willit

Detective Williams

Ralph Redman

I have notes from Tic Tac on who saw each person last, and for all but Ralph it was a co-worker. I write those names down as well. For Ralph, the last person is complicated, considering his open courtroom suicide.

From there I move to anyone with a connection to the case. Of course, all family members who I know of get a card, now, and as they are discovered. That isn't many people which is probably intentional. Killers don't like complications. Big families mean complications. I have a list of friends and close co-workers not already indexed that all get cards. For now, I also include Mia's boyfriend, North Madison, Thomas Miller, our creepy forensic guy, and every person on our team, even the meek little girls. Then there's Houston, Murphy, Roger, Kane, and even me, as all of us have something to do with this case and might connect a dot. Kane through me. Perhaps me through Roger.

I pin them all up on the board and pick up my ice cream, staring at the names, which usually triggers ideas and revelations, but I get nothing. I do have a moment when I consider Murphy's worries over my ex-partner, and I consider giving him a card, but right now, he's not yet involved. As for him being a suspect, he knows me well. He's well connected to me, and he even knows Roger, but Greg is in his early thirties, and I reject him as a possibility. He's not this guy. I know him.

Greg is not the Umbrella Man.

The end.

CHAPTER TWENTY-SIX

Setting Greg aside as a suspect, I consider others. And I keep considering. I'm a whole lot of blank space. I wonder how the dumb people in the world survive the blank space. It's fucking suffocating. I need to make something happen. I write out another card: *The Umbrella Man.*

I pin that on its own board. I then start writing a card for every word that comes to my mind about this monster; it's what I call my rapid-fire process, freeform, wild in the wilderness. If I write it, it stays. Whatever comes to mind, no matter how illogical it may seem, stays on the list. And so, I begin:

Asshole
Stalker
Creep
Smart
Genius
Manipulator
Evil
Law enforcement
Small dick
Short man
Big ego
Control freak
Insecure
Confident
Lean
Fit
Strong
Skilled with weapons
Knowledge of the press
Little bitch, not to be confused with little dick
Single white asshole
No tattoos

Good looking but short (this would rule out Thomas and Houston, but I still want both on the list)

Over forty

Educated

OCD

The OCD reminds me of Tic Tac's assignment to find out about the victims, so I finish off a bite of ice cream and call him. He doesn't answer, and I toss down my phone.

I grab all the papers from the printer and make stacks by name on the floor. That's what I do. I make a lot of stacks. I make a lot of lists. I pace and stare at the stacks and lists. And I eat, in this case, I eat ice cream and stare at the stacks. Frustrated, I end up *just* eating ice cream because I can think of nothing. Nothing. Holy fuck, I have nothing. I'm blank. I sit down on the floor in front of the stacks, ice cream still in route from the pint to my mouth, pint to mouth. Repeat, repeat—why the hell am I thinking of nothing helpful?

I rotate and look at the names on the board, and there are only two over forty: Murphy and Roger. It's not either one of them. I lay down, and I repeat those names: Murphy and Roger. This mental block is about Roger, I decide, being objective about myself. I don't want to deal with him. I don't want to face him. I don't want him to see the killer I see when I look in the mirror but I have to find a way to remove him from the picture, at least mentally.

There's a sound downstairs, and most likely, it's Kane, but for good measure, I grab my weapon and set it on my belly, trying to stay focused but ready to shoot anyone who isn't Kane. Umbrella Man clearly has a fixation on me. He went through Murphy and Roger to get to me. Logically, this could be about Roger or even Murphy, but the common denominator is me.

There's a sound by the door, and I glance over to find Kane crossing the room. I sit up, and he kneels in front of me, his jacket and tie gone, those brown eyes so black they could drag me to hell, and I'm pretty sure I'd burn there willingly.

"Are you planning to shoot me this time, Lilah?"

"Are you planning to give me a reason?"

"I thought I already did?"

"True. Very true." I set the gun aside. "But not now. Now, I'm thinking. This case is all about me, Kane. Whoever this is has to be in law enforcement. They know things about me that makes that assumption logical. This person must have watched my career. This person knows forensics. And they managed to get rid of evidence I bagged at a scene. It just didn't make it to the station. They know *me*. That means they know *you*."

"What if it's not law enforcement at all? Who else has been watching you just like they watched your mother?"

"Pocher? You think he hired someone to do this?"

"You did when you called me after the first murder."

"I know, but I can't let the Society become my fall guy for all cases."

"And you can't ignore them in this one, not right after I threatened them. Not when I targeted Pocher's brother."

"You had him kidnapped and then played hero and saved him. He knew you had him kidnapped. You wanted him to know. He can't prove it but he knew."

"Your point?"

"Which was supposed to back them off, not ignite another attack. He's afraid of you, Kane. The more I think about this being the Society, the less likely that feels."

"It's a game of chess. We can't assume to know their next move. That's dangerous."

A thought hits me. "What about Pocher's brother?" I scoot to my knees, facing him. "Who is he? What is he? Could he be crazy and being kidnapped sent him over the edge?" I hold up a hand. "No. It doesn't matter. Don't answer. I'm losing it. I'm reaching. I don't have my head in the game. I'm all over the place right now." I catch myself on his knees and try to get up, but I never make it. Kane catches my legs.

"You have Roger in your head, Lilah," he accuses, because Kane knows me, he knows my fears. "Did you see him?"

"He's still in Connecticut handling another case."

"He can't see what's not there."

"It is there. I'm there for him to see."

"You aren't me, Lilah, I won't ever let that happen."

"We both know I'm already there."

"No. You're not already there. Trust me."

"Because I now know that you'll bury a body for me if I need you to?"

"Yes, Lilah. And it's time we both said that out loud. Because I will bury a fucking body for you."

"Are we really going to fucking go there, Kane?"

"It's about damn time we did, don't you think?"

My cellphone rings. "That's going to be Tic Tac and—"

"He can wait, but I can't. I'm not waiting. Not this time."

CHAPTER TWENTY-SEVEN

Kane and I sit there on our knees in the middle of Purgatory, two people who go to our knees for no one, and yet, here we are now together. That night is between us, and he's right; we can't dodge this. I knew that last night. My mind goes there now, and I can almost feel the ocean air washing over me. *Kane is holding my attacker. Blood and sand clump in my mouth from where my teeth have bitten into my tongue while my face has been shoved into the dirt. The drugs I've been given are blurring everything, except Kane holding that man, Kane who hasn't killed him yet. He's talking to him. My God he's talking to him. And then there's the blade in his belt, the one that I'm certain would have been used to kill me if Kane hadn't shown up. Everything just fades into desperation and anger, and somehow, I'm stabbing my attacker over and over and over again. I just can't make myself stop.*

I snap back to the present and grab Kane's shoulders. "I know you saved my life. In more ways than one. I don't know what I would have said or done if I would have called the police that night. I don't know what I would have become. Probably everything I don't want to become, but you know I could."

"No." He strokes my hair from my face and tilts my gaze to his. "I didn't let that happen."

"I'm still angry at you for that night."

"I didn't get there in time. I didn't stop him from raping you. I didn't get him the hell out of there fast enough. I didn't kill him fast enough. I will never let you down like that again."

"So is that what we're doing? Blaming you?"

"I'm okay with the blame, Lilah. I'm not okay without you." His mouth closes down on mine, and suddenly, there is nothing but me and this man. We tug at our clothing. We tug at each other's hair. We end up naked in the middle of the floor on top of all of my paperwork, and it's as it used to be with Kane. There are no more walls. There are no more barriers. We have no inhibitions. We roll to our sides. He rolls to his back. We end up in the chair with me on top of him, and I swear I yank a chunk of his hair out and that man moans like it's pleasurable. When it's all said and done, somehow, we're back on the floor, naked, side by side, and leaning on the chair we were in a few minutes before.

I lay on his shoulder, and somehow, a part of my life that almost destroyed me, is a softer shade of ugly, at least the part that affected me with this man. But with that dulling, another knife has been sharpened. "In the back of my mind," I say, "there's been this question I haven't wanted to speak out loud."

"About your father?" he asks, and we turn to face each other.

"Yes. I keep thinking about that moment when I told him the Society had me raped, and he told me I was lucky they didn't kill me. The plan was to kill me. I knew it was, I believed it was."

"As did I."

"Did my father know? And did he know they were going to kill my mother? Because Kane, I know they did. *I know it.*" I don't give him time to answer. "If I find out that he did, I'm going to need you to kill him for me. I'll have to ask you to kill him for me."

His expression hardens, and he grabs the blanket on the chair and pulls it around me. "He's your father. We won't come back from that. Don't ask me to do something we can't survive."

"If you don't do it, I will, and I won't come back from that. You know I won't."

"We'll get the truth, and we'll make decisions when we do, together."

"Maybe we can just have him drugged and raped." My cellphone rings, and I jolt. "I forgot it was ringing earlier. I have to get it." Kane stretches to grab it from the desk before handing it to me.

We share a look that punches with history before he stands and starts pulling on his pants. I glance at Tic Tac's number and answer. "Oh, thank God. I called you three times."

"Did something happen?"

"I talked to Mia's boyfriend. He's a photographer. He was on a shoot out of town, and he said he couldn't reach her. He was worried, but they kind of had an on again off again relationship, so he thought she decided off was permanent. He said she wasn't really messy, but she never hung her clothes up. She'd try them on and throw them onto the floor."

That doesn't fit the OCD shape of her apartment at all. "What else?"

"Her boss said she called in sick the day before she disappeared."

Because Umbrella Man had her already. He probably made her clean her own place. "What else?"

"Shelly's parents are overseas, and no one can reach them. It's causing some concern."

"Oh shit. Get with the Texas officials and have them do a safety check at their home. Do it now."

"On it. I'll call you back, but oh crap. Crap. Crap. Crap."

"Fuck me, Tic Tac. Crap what?"

"I'm looking at a report I pulled. I tracked Detective Williams' cellphone pings for the past month. She was on Mia Moore's street a week before she died."

"Holy fuck. Call for that wellness check and call me back."

Kane is sitting at my desk drinking my cold coffee. He arches a brow. I rush toward him and motion for him to let me sit. "Problem?"

"A big one," I say, grabbing the NYPD investigation file from my briefcase because I don't remember anything about Mia calling in sick to work in that data.

I flip through pages, and it's not there. Nothing about Mia being out sick. That would be part of a basic interview done in the twenty-four hours following an incident, and Mia's boss was contacted. If he told Tic Tac, he would have told us. It was that research girl, Lily, who talked to him. I go through my records, find her number, and call her. Kane walks out of the room and disappears into the apartment. I sit down. "Lily," I say when she answers. "This is Agent Love. Did you talk to Mia Moore's boss?"

"Yes, I did. I wrote a report on the call."

"Who instructed you to do that if Detective Williams was missing in action?"

"It's a standard process. I create the lists of contacts. I do preliminary phone interviews. Detective Williams follows up in person. We've done this for dozens of cases."

"Were you told that Mia Moore was out sick the day before her murder?"

"No," she says, a lift to her voice. "Her boss said no such thing to me."

She's lying, I think. "He told my office but not you?" I challenge.

"Maybe he was hiding it, and the FBI label scared him into talking? Do you want me to research him a bit more?"

"No. I want you to find Williams."

"I don't know where she is."

Just like she doesn't know where my missing evidence is. She or Williams took it. The question is why? I don't believe her. I dial Houston. He answers on the first ring. "Agent Love."

"Lily just lied to me, and Williams was on Mia Moore's street the week she died."

"Lily is afraid of her own shadow. Maybe she's afraid of Williams?"

"I don't know. Maybe. None of this makes sense. Maybe she's working for our dear friends."

"Dear friends. Check. Murphy made that association clear. As to Lily working for them: with what endgame?"

"I don't know. I don't fucking know. Watch her and watch your back."

"Does that mean we're on the same team now?" he challenges.

"It means watch your back." I hang up.

Kane walks in and sets a steaming cup of coffee in front of me, holding another in his hand. "Breakthrough?"

"From my perspective, the evidence points to Detective Williams being the Umbrella Man."

"But you don't believe the evidence," he assumes.

"No. I don't even come close to believing the fucking evidence."

"Tell me about it. Maybe I can pull some whispers from the wind."

"You and your damn connections, Kane. You're a criminal."

"You want to tell me about it?"

"Yes. I want to tell you about it, asshole."

He laughs and motions to the chairs. My cellphone rings with Tic Tac's number again. "They're dead. It looks like a double suicide."

"Get me a number for whoever's in charge. Text it to me." I disconnect. "The second victim's parents in Texas were found dead in an apparent double suicide. Detective Williams' boyfriend killed himself in an apparent suicide today."

"Are we going to Texas?"

"We?"

"I own the chopper. I'll give you a ride with me inside the chopper."

"That's bribery."

"And?"

"And we're not going to Texas."

He arches a brow. "Why not?"

"Because Detective Williams is going to show up dead here." A thought hits me. "Or Lily. Umbrella Man is getting people to do work for him by threatening people close to them." I walk around the desk and hand Kane my coffee. I squat and find the information sheet on Lily, key in her address into my phone, and then holster my gun that is still on the ground before I stand up.

"I have to go to Lily's place now."

CHAPTER TWENTY-EIGHT

Lily isn't one of the bad guys. She's one of the victims. I need to save her.

I start for the door, determined to get to her now, quickly, but I stop dead, turning to face Kane. "No. Going to Lily's is a rash, wrong move. I need to think."

"Think out loud," Kane urges, stepping closer to me again. "Tell me what you know. Lily works with Detective Williams, correct?"

I scowl at him. "You know things you shouldn't know, Kane Mendez."

"Irrelevant at the moment. Think out loud."

"Okay," I say. "First, Umbrella Man. I believe he has OCD. I even believe he makes his victims clean up their own living and work spaces under the threat of some sort of pain, but that's speculation."

"Based on what?"

"The crime scenes. The living space of the victims is sparkling clean, completely outside of a average living condition. We now know that wasn't normal for the victims." I walk away from him, thinking as I talk, recapping what I already believe I know. "He's white," I turn to face him, "in his forties, fit, white-collar, smart. My profile. More speculation. I think he's high level law enforcement, someone Murphy's level."

His lips quirk, and he motions to my board where the index cards are pinned. "And he has a small dick."

"That is not a joke. Did you know that the Golden State Killer had an abnormally small dick? He dominated and raped women, and he especially liked ones with large men in their lives he could force to watch."

149

"I did *not,* in fact, know that the Golden State Killer had an abnormally small dick. This is why I love you, Lilah. I'm always just a little more educated with you in my life."

"Kane," I warn. "I'm being serious."

His brown eyes dance with mischief. "As am I. Keep going."

"I believe that the women he killed aren't his only victims. He plays with the people around them. Call them secondary victims to the primary ones. All speculation but I'm working the theory that he tells them that if they don't do something for him, he'll kill someone they love. And then, somehow, he gets them to kill themselves. Maybe to save their loved ones. Maybe to save themselves a worse fate. Ultimately, he still kills his primary target."

"How were they killed?"

"We believe the primary victims to have been poison, but we're struggling to find the toxin. Suicide for the secondary victims." My brows dip, this conversation bringing a hot point to my mind. "Ralph Redman. He's a secondary victim connected to one of the primaries. He killed himself in open court. His place wasn't spotless. I'm guessing the Texas crime scene where we have the double suicide won't be either. I think," I pause in thought and continue as my ideas materialize, "the secondary victims aren't worthy of his hyper-focus. They're like the pig he killed for the blood." At that point, I recap everything, including my theory that the blood in the fan was simulating rain.

I summarize it all with, "I now believe that Lily, who works as a staff member of the NYPD, might be one of the secondary victims."

"And who's the primary?"

"Detective Williams, though I'm not sure why Lily would be emotionally attached to Detective Williams. Maybe they're lovers. That actually makes sense. They could be a couple. Damn, Williams must be gay. Or maybe Lily's a niece. I need to find out. I'm better with killers than I am normal people and their love lives."

"I thought Ralph was her boyfriend?"

"Right. Okay. She's not a lesbian." I shrug. "Okay, well, maybe she's bi."

"Or maybe Lily's not a girlfriend."

"Yeah, maybe, but that's not as romantic, now is it?"

"And you are, of course, so romantic?"

I frown. "I can be romantic."

His lips curve. "Can you now?"

"I can. Remember your birthday the year before I left?"

His voice softens. "But you left, Lilah."

"That doesn't erase the good times."

"Is that right?"

"Now you're clearly baiting me to say what you want. I baked you a cake. I don't bake. That's romantic." I sit on the edge of the desk. Kane claims the spot next to me while I shift back to the case. "If I go grab Lily, it seems to me that he might kill Williams."

"I think that's a reasonable assumption," Kane agrees, shifting topics with me, without so much as a blink. "Why don't we have my men watch Lily?"

I push off the desk and step in front of him. "I'm pulling a lot of your resources."

"And that's a problem why?"

"That problem you told me about," I say, thinking of his uncle. "Isn't that where your focus needs to be?"

"I'm capable of multitasking in all ways, Lilah, or I'd be dead already."

"Are you trying to convince me that you are or are not your father with that statement?"

"I'm not my father, but I am my father's son." His voice hardens and he repeats what he told me in his office. "I can't change that fact. You know that."

"I do know that," I say, a realization coming to me. "What I also know is that you've changed. You used to deny it all. Even when I got back into town, you weren't your father or your father's son. Now, you're at least admitting the part we both know we can't escape."

A muscle in his jaw flexes. "Call Jay. Tell him what you need." He pushes off the desk. "And I'll trade our coffee in for something stronger." He walks away, and I'm living a déjà vu moment from our past, when I knew that he was dealing with cartel business, and I pushed him about it. He'd shut me out, he'd push me back. Which was almost as bad as the times I knew he was dealing with cartel business and we both pretended I didn't. I don't know how to make this work with us, and yet, I'm ready to admit that I don't know how to *not* make it work anymore either. Right now, though, I just need to focus on Umbrella Man before he kills again.

By the time Kane returns, I'm on the floor in front of the chair with a fluffy rug beneath me, and I've just finished up a call with Jay. Kane sets a glass of wine on the table next to me. He then claims the chair opposite the table and opens his MacBook; another déjà vu moment. This is what we did. I worked. He worked. We were always together.

"Any problems with Jay?" he asks.

"Not with Jay. I've already established my dominant alpha role with him."

Kane laughs. "I have no doubt."

My phone rings on the table with what I am certain is a Texas number. I move to the chair and answer the call that is, in fact, the lead law enforcement officer handling the crime scene for Shelly's parents. "This is relevant to a case we're currently working," I say. "What is the condition of the house? Messy? Immaculate? Average?"

Officer Wright is quick to answer. "Average to messy." Considering Ralph's nasty toilet, we've now confirmed that the suicide victims do not receive the same one-on-one personal attention from Umbrella Man which I still believe is about worth. He doesn't find them worthy of his time.

"How long have they been dead?"

"I'm no medical examiner but I've been around the track. Three days at least." They died before their daughter. That has my mind racing and I quickly finish up the call.

I sit there a moment and consider what I've just learned. Ralph killed himself and Williams is missing. If she ends up dead, the suicides taking place before the murders, supports my theory that he taunts the loved ones of the victims before killing the victims themselves. But if that's true, who did he taunt before he killed Mia? There may be a body we have yet to discover. I quickly dial Houston and follow that with a call to Tic Tac. We're now looking for another body and anyone who traveled to Texas recently who is on our list.

Through all of this, Kane works on some sort of financial project for his oil business which I know because he shares a few details about a new drill site he's launching in between my calls. But Kane doesn't interrupt my process. He understands me and my Purgatory, in ways Rich never could fathom. Rich couldn't handle how dark I get in this place. Kane can handle anything. We don't work unless he knows that I can, too.

It's late, well after midnight, when my work slows, and I turn my attention to Kane. He feels my stare and looks down at me, where I've settled on the floor again, and as he always does, just that quickly, I'm his full focus. He sets his MacBook aside. "What do you want to ask me, Lilah?"

"Who did your uncle have killed?"

The air shifts, his mood darker, but he doesn't pull away. He never pulls away. He stares at me a moment and then takes my hand and guides me to his chair and scoots over, giving me room to join him. I sit down next to him, and he meets my gaze before he says, "I know that I told you that if you asked, I'd answer, but you don't want to know, Lilah. And I don't want to tell you."

"You can trust me."

"It's not about trust, beautiful. You know enough about me to destroy me if you wanted to, and even when we were apart, I knew that would never happen."

"If it's not about trust, what then?"

"That promise I made you earlier. I promised that I wouldn't let you become what you could become, what my world could make you if we let it. When you start crossing certain lines with me, that's what will happen."

I'm not sure if he believes that or if he fears that I'll hate him if I know all that he is and can be. I did shut him out after he buried that body, and by doing so, I gave him every reason to assume that in the right circumstances, I will judge him as a monster. "I'm not going to push you now, but you say that I save you. I can't do that if you don't give me the chance."

"You do, Lilah. You are the only thing that saves me."

"Then in your silence and mine alike, you find acceptance from me for that life that isn't there."

"Without it, I find hate," he says, confirming what I'd just assumed.

"No. I *promise you* that is not the case. Make yourself tell me. That will force you to limit yourself."

"Lilah—"

"If you want me to stay, Kane, we both know that I can't let you stay silent. We both know that the middle isn't me pretending to be in the dark."

He stands up and takes me with him, his hand under my hair at my neck. "There is no if, Lilah. You're staying."

"I'm trying to save you."

"You save me *by staying*."

"Would you rather me imagine what you're doing, than you just telling me?"

"Yes," he says, without hesitation, and then he kisses me. "Yes, I would."

In other words, he believes that nothing I can imagine is as bad as reality. He kisses me then and I let him, and in that kiss, I remember now what I've failed to remember since the night of my attack. When Kane kisses me, he always kisses me like he needs me to save him, while I always kiss him like I'm hoping he'll destroy me.

CHAPTER TWENTY-NINE

I wake in a bed I once said I would never sleep in again, pressed close to a man who is the devil incarnate, but apparently, I still love that devil. My cellphone is also ringing, so I roll over and grab it, answering without even looking at the caller ID. "Agent Love."

"Agent. I can't get used to that title."

At the sound of Roger's voice, I sit straight up. "Roger." Crap. My voice sounds like someone shoved a damn banana in my mouth and said eat it all now. Fuck. Fuck. Fuck. Kane is immediately next to me, grabbing my leg and grounding me. God, this man knows me. "Are you back in the city?"

"I am, and I hear I'm reporting to you on this case."

"I don't think you need to report to me, but I've got this one."

"You've got this one?" he challenges, sounding quite peeved. "Why wouldn't you use me? One of our own is missing. Why don't we meet for coffee? We can talk it out."

"Are you at the station today?" I ask.

"I am."

"I'll find you there."

"I'm shocked you don't want to have coffee. We're old friends. You're like a daughter, Lilah."

"I have a meeting. I'll find you."

"Huh. Yeah. You do that." He hangs up.

I scoot to the side of the bed and grab Kane's work shirt, pulling it on. By the time I have it wrapped around me, he's standing in front of me in his pants. "You're making this worse than it has to be. Go have coffee. Get it over with."

"I don't want to go to coffee with that man."

"Take me with you."

"What? Take you with me? You're suing the NYPD and the FBI."

His hands come down on my arms. "The department has a hard-on for me. They believe I'm a kingpin. He'll obsess over me and focus less on you."

"No. Absolutely not. I don't need Kane Mendez to hold my fucking hand. Seriously, Kane? Do you think I'm a toddler?"

"You're human, Lilah. You fear that man."

"I fear me. Just me. I don't need to share that with anyone but you. And I can do that, because you're just as scared of you as I am of me."

"But I don't fear him." He releases me. "But maybe that's the lesson here. I don't fear him. I embrace who I am. Embrace who you are, Lilah. That's why you're good at what you do. Because you see the evil out there. You understand it."

"Because I'm evil?"

"Because you're *you*. Look him in the eye and see that as the fucking advantage it is. You could ruin him if you wanted to. He can't ruin you."

"You hate him," I remind him. "That affects your opinions. You hated him from the moment you met him."

"He doesn't sit well in my gut. I use caution with those people."

"And yet you want me to go sit across from him?"

"Get past it," he pushes. "You're giving away your power and that's not like you."

I inhale and let it out. "You're right. God, I hate when you're fucking right." I grab my phone to call Roger back.

"I'll go pour the coffee I put on the timer," Kane says, walking toward the bedroom door.

My phone rings in my hand with an unknown number, and I answer, "Agent Love."

"Agent Love," an all-business female voice greets, "this is Melanie Carmichael. I'm the new medical examiner dealing with a number of murders that you're investigating. I think we should meet."

"Agreed. When?"

"When can you stop by?"

"I'll be there before lunch."

"That works."

We say our goodbyes, and I dial Roger. "Lilah?"

"I moved my meeting. I have a small window, depending on when and where we go. I need to stop by the medical examiner's office. Pick someplace in between there and the station."

"I'll come to you. How about Misty's Diner in forty-five minutes? That's right near your travels."

And it's his favorite place. Whatever, I guess. "That works." I say, hanging up to find Kane walking back into the bedroom with two cups of coffee in his hand.

He hands me a cup. "Got your meeting?"

"Thank you," I say, lifting my cup because I have manners despite often being told otherwise. "And yes. In forty-five minutes."

"Don't forget we have your father's fundraiser tonight."

My eyes go wide. "We declined."

"We didn't decline. We're going."

"Kane, you're suing the entire fucking legal system."

"Seems like an appropriate time to say hello, don't you think?"

"We're not going for you to say fuck you to law enforcement. I am law enforcement."

"And Murphy knows you're with me, Lilah. Own who you are. We were engaged. They all know us as a couple."

Were engaged. Why does that "were" punch me in the fucking gut so badly? "Kane—"

"The Society needs to see us together, and they need to see you behaving and supporting your father because we need them to back the fuck off. We destroy our powerful enemies by making them let their guard down."

"I don't even have a dress here or time to buy one."

He sets his cup down and then takes mine and does the same. "Come with me," he says, catching my hand in his, leading me through a wet dream of a bathroom, that I really fucking adore, to the giant closet, that I love just as much. My gaze goes left to my old side of the closet, and I suck in a breath; all of my clothes are still here.

I turn to Kane. "You didn't get rid of them?"

"No, Lilah. I didn't get rid of them."

"That must have been a bitch to explain to other women."

"We picked this place together. I didn't bring other women here. And there's a substantial amount of new items in the bags on the floor and hanging with tags. I had that personal shopper you like bring it all yesterday, including all your favorite toiletries."

I don't bring up the money. He's rich. I am too because of my mother's trust. It's not about the money to him or me. We've never had to have that between us. "You just assumed you'd get me back here."

"You belong here. You know it. I know it. Why are we going to pretend otherwise? That apartment you moved into was wasted money."

"Kane, *my job*. I can't just—"

He pulls me to him hard and fast. "Murphy knows," he bites out. "Fuck the rest of them. I told you. You're staying."

"That's my decision, not yours. You can't command me, Kane."

His lips press together. "You're right." His voice is as tight as his expression. "Make your own fucking decision, Lilah. I'll shower at the office." He releases me and walks out of the closet.

"Fuck."

I turn and look at the clothes, and there's a pink dress with tags on it turned this direction. It's obviously a dress Kane wanted me to notice. I walk over to it and catch the silk in my hands. He's the only person who sees the part of me that is softer, that is pink and like my mother. And yet, he's the only person who sees that dark horrible part of me as well. That matters. Fuck. It matters. I turn and run out of the closet, darting through the bathroom. "Kane?! Kane?!"

He doesn't answer, but when I step into the bedroom, he's sitting on the bed. "I fucking love you," I blurt. "Is that what you want to hear?"

He stands up. "And what else, Lilah?"

"We'll go to the party."

"And?"

"And you're such a demanding bastard. I'm not leaving. Is that what you want to hear? But don't read into that. I love this apartment and bathroom and—"

He's now in front of me, cupping my head. "You're not leaving. Yes. That's what I want to hear. You can stop there."

"You're still an asshole."

"I know." He kisses me. That's what assholes do. They kiss you, and you forget why their asshole-ness matters. But I'll remember. He knows I'll remember.

CHAPTER THIRTY

I'm late for coffee, which only proves Kane is an asshole. He wouldn't let me out of the fucking shower. I didn't even get to admire all the tile work I had picked out because he was all over me the entire time. Fuck. My hair is still damp, so now it's going to be a frizzy mess all day, which, you know, I guess works if it somehow makes me less approachable.

After a short walk from the apartment, I step to a corner and stare at the Misty's Diner sign. My cellphone rings with Kane's number. "Just do it," he says when I answer.

"Are you watching me? Seriously, Kane? I can't live with a stalker."

"Lilah, I'm not watching you. I just know you."

"You don't know me as well as you think." I hang up. I hate being predictable and readable. I hate being a little fucking wuss who sucks her thumb in the corner because Old Man Smokey is here, and he might hurt my feelings by seeing that I'm an evil bitch. I cross the road, and I don't stop this time. I enter the semi-full diner and scan for Roger. He's not here, damn it. Now I have to sit in a booth and suck my wuss ass thumb and wait on him.

The hostess motions for me to claim a seat. I grab a spot to the right of the door by a window. My back is to that window, but I can see the door and the diner. As long as I don't get shot in the back, all is peachy. Well, except for the fact that my old mentor is about to look in my eyes and most likely see a killer. And cough on me. God, I hate those coughs. It's really rather odd to me how a man that anal has such a dirty habit. It doesn't compute.

Ten minutes pass, and I finally get some damn coffee, and it doesn't even have pumpkin in it. Mother of God, thank fuck for that. Roger hasn't shown up, so I try to call him. The connection goes straight to voicemail. My cellphone rings, and I glance down to where it rests on the table to find Tic Tac calling. "Yes, Master Tic Tac. Or are you the submissive and Mike's the master?"

"We're gay, Lilah, not kinky."

"Oh. I'm so sorry. You know you can still change that. If you just—"

"Stop," he bites out. "Stop talking."

"Fine. I was just trying to help you spice things up."

"I have an idea. A work idea."

"Is it a good one?" I ask.

"It's going to be one of those days with you, isn't it?"

I sip my coffee. "Looks like it."

"I'm going to take every person who has even the slightest connection to any of this, even the Texas suicides, and link cell towers, job histories, and even places they visit. It's going to take time, but I talked to Murphy, and he's getting me a team to help."

"How long will this take with the team?"

"We'll break it down in chunks and extract information as we go. It's all a matter of homing in on what key information, and finding what matters in the middle of all the junk."

"Do we have *anything* that matters right now? It sure as fuck doesn't feel like it."

"Agreed, which is why I'm doing this. And by the way, I'm now on your task force, extra motivated to put up with your crap by way of a big raise."

"Oh, Fuck. I asked him to get someone else."

He grunts. "Seriously, Lilah? Can you not just keep things to yourself?"

"I'm joking. Welcome to Team Love, otherwise known as Team Torture."

"It's hard to tell when you're joking, Lilah."

"It's my smooth operator, undercover skills. Have someone on that new team of yours get me a list of hard-to-identify toxins, pronto."

"Yes, Agent Love," he says, all monotone and robot-like.

"You should be the submissive."

He hangs up. I laugh and dial Jay. "Anything?"

"Lily went to work, stopped at Starbucks on the way there, and seems like a fairly normal person, but who am I to judge? I know people like you and Kane."

"You're just so fucking funny. What else?"

"We went into her apartment and it's normal, too."

"Was her bed made?"

"What?" he asks, and my gaze lifts as a familiar Hispanic woman in a waitress uniform appears behind the counter. Her eyes meet mine and recognition comes to both of us. She's the guard from the morgue. I disconnect my call and stand up to approach her. She turns and starts running, turning into the kitchen. I try to lift the counter door, but it's stuck. I go over the fucking thing and take a few plates and glasses with me, but fuck it. People scream. I carry on. I pull my gun and enter the kitchen to find two people in aprons looking terrified. "Where'd she go?"

They point to the back of the building, and I rush that way and down a hallway that exits to an alleyway. She's not there. Gone. Vanished. But in the center of the walkway is something that looks to be pink. I frown and walk in that direction. I squat down and stare at the gift that was left for me. It's a rubber pig. I understand the message that I don't believe most would. It means that I'm proving as inconsequential as the pig. I'm not performing to standard. He might as well gut me and bleed me dry. Sirens sound in the background, and I sigh. Fuck. Now I have to deal with this bullshit. I bag the pig and shove it in the field bag that's always at my hip.

The manager of the diner meets me at the door. A police cruiser pulls up, and the officers rush in our direction. I flash my badge. "Agent Love. Part of an ongoing investigation. Stand down." I look at the manager. "Who was the woman I just chased?"

"Maria Mendez."

At Kane's surname, he has my attention; though, it is a common name. "I need her contact information and quickly."

"Yes, ma'am."

I turn to the officers. "Tall, Hispanic female about one-fifty. Search the perimeter."

They nod and take off. I meet the manager at the back door, and he hands me a piece of paper with the address on it. "She doesn't have a phone."

"How long has she worked here?"

"Six months. She's a good employee. She has little kids."

"Okay." I use my manners again. I'm on a roll. "Thanks. Sorry for the mess." I reach in my bag and hand him a few hundred dollars I keep for just such an occasion. "That's for the coffee."

His eyes go wide. "Thank you. Thank you so much."

I start walking. I know this city from my time with the NYPD. The address is only a few blocks away. I dial Kane. "How bad was it?"

"Do you know a woman named Maria Mendez, thirtyish, one hundred and fifty pounds, really good at making a bitch scowl?"

"That doesn't ring a bell but we Mexicans love a surname a million deep. Why?"

"I'll tell you later. I need to deal with this."

"Roger?"

"No show."

"That's odd."

"Yeah. It is, isn't it? I need to go." I hang up and scan the streets. I make the walk to Maria's in five minutes, and I follow a tenant into the buzzer-driven door. I'm about to head up the stairs when Maria steps out from under the stairwell.

"I needed the money. I have kids. One of them is sick. He needs special breathing treatments, and I was desperate." She starts to cry. "I got scared when I saw you, but I can't run. I don't want to run. My kids need me, though. They need me." She sobs.

Fuck. I hate tears. "Tell me everything," I say, a phrase that usually makes people think I know anyway. It works.

"He wanted me to pretend to be a guard and sneak in and take photos of a few medical reports."

"He who?"

"Some reporter." She hugs herself. "I don't know what website. It was a website."

"How did you meet him?"

"He came into the diner and heard me talking about my kid to a regular customer."

"What did he look like?"

"He was early thirties, black, new fancy suit. He didn't know, but he still had a tag on it. Didn't give me a name."

That wasn't Umbrella Man. It was probably some guy he pulled off the street. This is all a setup. I was supposed to find her. I was supposed to find the pig. And if I walk away and leave this woman, he'll kill her to torment me. It's all a game. He's making me chase my tail. "I don't want you to stay here. I want you to go out of town. I'm sending someone to pick you up. I'll pay for everything."

"What about my job?"

"Is there someplace you want to live other than here?"

"Well, Colorado. I heard it's cheap to live there."

"Colorado it is. I'll give you enough money to start over."

"Really?"

"Really. Go pack. I'll arrange it all."

She throws her arms around me and hugs me. Tears and a hug, shoot me now. When I'm released, she takes off, and I step outside and call Jay. "No, she did not make her bed, and why is that important?"

"Habits define character, but right now, I have a situation." I make the arrangements for Maria Mendez. I don't think that last name is an accident. It's a message I was meant to receive when I found Maria. She is nothing in the big picture. He's telling me that Kane is nothing. He's telling me that Kane can't protect me, like I need Kane's fucking protection.

That said, I still haven't heard from Roger, and I'm now worried. Was Maria a distraction and Roger the target? I dial him again, and the line rings, and Roger picks up. "Sorry, Lilah. My damn subway stalled. It was hell down there. Are we still having coffee? I'm a few blocks away."

We are most definitely not having coffee. "I'll find you later."

"I'll meet you at the medical examiner's office."

Of course he will, because I just can't escape this man or apparently the Umbrella Man. "Fine." I disconnect, but I don't start walking. Something niggles at me and then begins to claw. There is something right in front of my face that I'm missing. Something about this morning and these events. And what I miss, with this asshole, could cost a life.

CHAPTER THIRTY-ONE

While walking to the medical examiner's office, I dial Tic Tac. "I need that list of toxins."

"I emailed it and included signs to look for that might indicate exposure."

"Thanks," I say, and I'm about to hang up but he isn't done talking.

"Wait," he says. "You said thanks?"

I don't reply. I hang up and dial Kane. "Talk to me, beautiful."

"That Maria Mendez situation. It was a message to me about you. I'll spare you the details as to why I say that. He really might come at you, Kane."

"We had this conversation. Let's hope he does."

"Stop being an arrogant asshole who thinks he's invincible. A rival gang might not get to you, but this man, he's different. He's smart. He's sneaky. He's not what you expect. Take precautions. I'm not playing with you on this Kane. He likes toxins. That's hard to defend."

"He's rattling you."

"I don't like when these things get personal. You're personal."

"Where are you right now?"

"A block from the medical examiner's office. I'm meeting the new medical examiner on this case, *and* Roger is meeting me there."

"Which explains your current state of mind. I'll meet you there and take you to lunch."

"No. I need to go to the station when this is done. I'll grab something on my way. Just—be careful."

"Lilah—"

I disconnect before he tries to coddle me and then I have to hurt him when I see him again. As it is, he's putting me in a pink dress and making me see my father and Pocher tonight. I like the dress but not the bullshit political event that I have to attend wearing it. I bring the medical facility into view, and in a near afterthought, pause, pulling up the email from Roger about his case. I step to a wall next to a restaurant and quickly scan the details, finding it uneventful as it relates to my cases. Right now, I'm going to focus on this case, not tonight and not on Roger.

With that affirmation in my mind, I cross the street and enter the building, making a beeline for the elevator. "Lilah!"

At the sound of Roger's voice, I stop dead and steel myself for the impact of looking at him, the impact of looking into his damn eyes. I give myself a pep talk: *Don't be a wimp ass bitch, Lilah.* Pep talks work. They motivate. Or so my mother used to tell me. I huff out a breath and turn to face the judge and jury. He steps in front of me, tall, thin, and fit, his skin wrinkled from age, sun, and cigarettes. His eyes, those piercing blues eyes that always undo people, give me a once over. "You look good, girl. Give me a hug." He opens his arms.

I don't move. "I don't hug, Roger. You know that about me."

He laughs. "I see LA didn't soften you up any."

"No. It didn't." I meet his stare, and I find I don't feel the intimidation I thought I'd feel. Roger rattles criminals. He doesn't rattle killers. We're too cold to be that easily affected. I forgot that fact. What I realize now, is that I just don't like the man, and admiration is no longer there to fill the void and I don't know why. Whatever the case, this is rather anticlimactic. "I need to get upstairs." I turn and start for the elevator.

He falls into step with me and starts coughing. I grind my teeth and endure. Once we're in the car, he glances over at me. "Any breaks in the case?"

"None that I'm ready to share," I say, something Roger will understand. I don't talk about what I think about. Well, except to Kane, but no one knows I talk to Kane.

He laughs. "I know how you work, but this one is really mine, babe. How about we work it together?"

I glance over at him. "In case I didn't tell you in the past, I don't like the babe thing. I get urges to lift my knee when someone calls me babe. And I don't play well with others. You know this about me, too."

"And yet, you enjoy the game the way I do. I'm sixty-four, Lilah. I'm retiring soon. Don't take the game away from me."

The elevator stops, and the doors open. I step into the hallway, and he joins me. "You're here. You can join me for this meeting, but I make no promises beyond that."

His eyes narrow on mine, something glinting in their depths that I can't name. "I used to be the person you came to on everything, and now, I do believe that you're territorial."

He's right, I am, and I'm not sure if that's about this case or still about me. It has to be about the defense mechanism he stirs in me. "Let's go talk to the medical examiner," I say, and I don't wait for a reply; I just start walking.

My cellphone rings, and it's the station number. "Agent Love."

"Agent Love, it's Thomas."

Creepy Thomas the forensics guy. This day just gets better and better. "Yes, Thomas?"

"Houston thought you'd want to know that we found matching unidentified male DNA at the scene of both crimes."

"What about at Ralph's place?"

"No. Nothing but him and Agent Williams."

Interesting. I don't think Umbrella Man goes to the secondary victims' homes. He wouldn't be able to tolerate leaving their houses dirty. Which means he hasn't been to Lily's house. So how does he communicate with them?

"On a separate note," Thomas says, reminding me he's still on the line. "You don't like me, do you?"

"I don't like anyone, Thomas. You fit right in. Do you need anything else?"

"You'll like Melanie. She knows what she's doing."

"And you know this how?"

"Exposure."

It's a weird answer. "Do you have anything else for me?"

"I guess not." He hangs up. For once, someone doesn't make me hang up first.

I motion Roger to the room that is our destination. "Was that news?" Rogers asks as we pause at the door.

"Forensics guy. Nothing helpful right now." It's not a lie; it's just not real information.

We enter the lab, and a tall, pretty black woman in a lab coat stands up. "Roger," she greets.

"Hi, Melanie," he says, greeting her. "Good to see you on this one." He motions to me. "This is Agent Love, FBI. She's my protégé and a good one she is."

"Nice to meet you, Agent Love," Melanie says, offering me her hand.

"What would be nice is for you to tell me you know the toxin that killed my victims."

She grimaces. "I wish I did."

I'm about to pull up the email that Tic Tac sent me when she reaches over to the lab table and slides a piece of paper in my direction. "That's a list of the toxins that are difficult, if not impossible to identify. We are deficient in equipment to find a few of these, but Beth will have access to that equipment when she arrives in Europe. We're just trying to get approval to send samples to her."

"I'll get you the approval," I say, picking up the list and noting the way she's given me ways these toxins could be used and acquired. I glance up at her. "You're efficient."

"Of course, I'm efficient. I'm the head medical examiner for the district. If protocol hadn't been broken, I would have handled this from the beginning. This is about lives lost. I take that seriously."

"What about the suicide victim, Ralph Redman? Are you familiar with that case?"

"I am. It's pretty cut and dry."

"Take another look. Pretend it's not."

"Okay." She looks confused. "What am I looking for?"

"What you're supposed to look for. Everything and anything. You called me. You obviously have my number.

Call me. Text me. Whatever. I'll get that sample transport approved." I glance at Roger. "What's your plan now?"

"I think I'll catch up with Melanie for a few minutes. You got time for lunch, Melanie?"

"I think I could swing that," she says.

I leave the room, and I'm bothered by Roger and Melanie having lunch for no reasonable reason other than that territorial thing he pointed out. I'm also bothered by that odd call from Thomas. I wait until I exit the building, and I call Murphy. "What can I do for you, Agent Love?"

"I need samples shipped to Europe. The lab here is having trouble getting it approved."

"Consider it approved. I'll handle it."

"Beth?"

"Just landed a few minutes ago. She's safe. What else?"

"I'm going to a fundraiser for my father tonight. That means our fucked-up friends will be there."

He laughs. "I don't remember that being our chosen phone nickname."

"I'm moving in with Kane."

"Did you need a house warming gift?"

"That's what you wanted, right? You get him through me?"

"It is a bonus, Agent Love."

"What don't I know about the two of you?" I ask the question I forgot to push Kane over last night.

"We have mutual enemies, and I like to keep my allies close."

"Kane is not your ally. It's a mistake to believe that."

"But he is yours. I have a meeting, Agent Love. Let me know if you need anything more." He disconnects, and I need to think again. That means I swing by the station, get a read on Lily, and then I'm going to head to Purgatory and get lost for a few hours until I'm trapped at that Godforsaken party. That niggling something is right there in my mind. If I can just get a damn pizza and some quiet, I'll grab it. I'll understand it.

CHAPTER THIRTY-TWO

I arrive at the station with the lunch hour fast approaching and go straight to Houston's office. Based on the conversation that includes words and phrases like "fuck," "bastard" and "are you serious?" he's apparently pissing someone off. He scowls at something said to him, glances up to lift a friendly finger at me, but quickly gets right back to pissing off the other person. While I appreciate his conversation skills, I really do, I leave. I don't have time to be entertained. I head to the elevator to travel down a level to the place where my new, but temporary, team works.

The car halts, and I step off to stand face to face with Thomas, who is still big, broad, and in my space currently giving me no room. "Personal fucking space again, Thomas," I snap. "Step back." He does. "And where are you going?"

"To piss."

"By way of an elevator?"

"There's a snack machine downstairs. I need a snack."

"A snack?"

"I have low blood sugar."

I scowl. "Is that a lie?"

"I don't lie."

"Okay, whatever. Take a piss. Get a snack. I don't care. Have everyone on our team give us a DNA sample including all the emergency and law enforcement that visited the locations of our crime scenes."

"They won't like that."

"Did I ask if they would like it?" I step around him.

"Agent Love."

I grimace and rotate to find him facing me now. "Yes, Thomas?"

"You think it's one of us?"

"Get me my samples, Thomas."

"Detective Williams still isn't back."

"I know."

"Her boyfriend killed himself."

"I know," I repeat.

"The parents of one of the victims killed themselves."

"You really didn't need to piss and eat a snack all that badly, did you?"

"A reporter cornered me this morning. She seemed to think Ralph killed those women, that this is all connected."

"Reporters are like the guy who says he loves you to get into your pants. They suck. Go take a piss, Thomas." I leave him there and walk down a hallway and into Detective Williams' office. It's, of course, empty. I walk to the desk and sit down. She's not dead yet. I'm sure of it. He has her. That bastard is saving her for me. She's going to end up an Umbrella Girl, and I haven't done nearly enough to figure out how the victims connect. Tic Tac is working that angle, but I need to look beyond the data. For that, Thomas gets a cookie. He got me focused on what's important in that connection.

Standing up, I exit the office, scanning the sea of desks, until I find Lily's workspace in a wall of cubicles, which is my destination. "What do you have for me, Lily?" I ask, claiming the chair by her desk.

"Agent Love." She sits up straighter. "I tried to reach the victim's parents to tell them Shelly was dead like you said, but they didn't answer. Someone else told them and—it must have gone badly. I think I would have known it went badly had it been me. I think I would have sent help. I'm good that way. I read people's voices. Now they're dead, but you're right; when it gets personal, you get motivated. And this feels personal." She holds up a pad of paper with a list of names. "I'm calling every person I can find who might connect our victims. I'm going to find something to help you catch this asshole."

"You didn't make those people kill themselves."

"Maybe if I would have called sooner. Maybe I should—"

"No. They were already dead. I talked to the officers on the scene. They'd been dead for days." I lean in closer. "I believe the killer uses the people close to a victim and forces them to do things by promising he won't hurt the people they love. And then, he tells them to kill themselves or they'll get to watch the people they love die."

Her eyes go wide. "Ralph killed himself. Are you saying—is Detective Williams next?"

"I believe she's still alive right now. We need to catch this guy. We need someone to tell us what they know because someone knows something. Who do you think that might be?"

"I don't know." She doesn't look away. She doesn't blink. "I can do research. That's my thing. I'm good at research. She's my boss, so I feel weird digging into her personal life, but I can. I want to help. I really want to help."

I know then that I'm wrong about her. She's not being held captive but that doesn't erase the fact that she lied to me the other night about what Mia Moore's boss told her. What the fuck is this? I need to think. I need to get to Purgatory. I stand up. "You have a new boss coming in soon. I'll let him direct you."

Houston pokes his head into the cubical and motions me down the hallway, and I follow him into a vacant office. "First off," he says, "your guy, Greg, won't call me back and Murphy axed that idea anyway. He said you already know that. Do you want me to just bring in my guy?"

Fucking Murphy. And fucking Greg. Even if Murphy got to him, he should at least be calling me back. "I'll talk to Greg and Murphy," I say. "Give me the weekend. I'll get back with you by Monday."

"Okay then, next, in about ten minutes, the mayor is going to claim in a press conference that Ralph's suicide was a tragic accident and that his focus will be on improving courthouse security. If he's questioned about the two murders, he's going to call them isolated and unrelated."

"Okay."

"Okay? I thought this was what you wanted. I thought you'd be happy."

"I might have been a bit too flippant on that topic. This is going to go badly, and you're going to get fired. It was nice working with you." I turn to leave and stop. "Damn it." I rotate to face him. "Murphy says I'm supposed to trust you and all that shit. Call the mayor."

"And say what?"

"Leave that to me."

"All right. I just hung up with him. He should answer." He makes the call, has a short exchange, and hands me the phone.

"Agent Love," the mayor greets.

"If we don't give the killer credit, he may lash out. If we do, he may lavish the attention and lash out. He's just that kind of bastard."

"How is he going to lash out?" he asks.

"He'll kill Detective Williams who I believe he's kidnapped. She's his prize. Unless she's him, which I doubt, but it's possible. Either way, you'll be blamed for her death because the killer will leak something about your mishandling causing this tragedy to the press."

"And you know this how?"

"It's what I do," I say. "You have to choose to trust me or not, but you're worried about how you look for political reasons. That tends to make people stupid. Don't be stupid."

"Stupid? Did you really just say that to me?"

"You have a serial killer in your city, Mayor. What did you want me to say? *Please make smart environmentally friendly choices.*"

"What are you advising, Agent Love?"

"I'd delay the press conference a few days and give us time to work. Of course, that's a risk. He's impatient for attention, but basically, we're fucked either way, so I'd wait. If he's pissed, he'll act out and that means we have a chance to catch him."

"He could kill again."

"And your press conference changes that how?"

"The press is going to leak this anyway," he argues. "I have to speak to them."

I shrug. "Okay."

"Okay?"

"It's your call. It's not mine. It's not Houston's. But consider my advice official FBI instructions. If you so choose to ignore them, that's also officially on you." I hang up and hand the phone to Houston.

He takes it, and I turn to leave.

"Lilah, damn it," he bites out. "Do not walk away."

"I need to work, Houston. I need to find Umbrella Man before he kills Williams."

"And I need to help you do it."

"Okay then. There was matching DNA found at both murder sites."

"Thomas told me."

"And I told Thomas to get me samples of everyone who was at those crime scenes and everyone who is working the cases. He's afraid to ask or just creepy. Or both. Either way, make sure he does it and send a team out to get samples from neighbors and co-workers and process them quickly."

"Fuck. I don't want to lose Williams."

This is one of those moments when people want me to say something encouraging or sympathetic. I don't do that. It's not natural. But hell, I try. "That would suck," I say, and with that valiant effort, I leave.

CHAPTER THIRTY-THREE

I decide I just need to run by the apartment I apparently rented for nothing at this point, and grab the small amount of things I have there. It's a quick trip and what strikes me during this visit is that I haven't heard from Junior. Could it be that Junior is Umbrella Man? It's possible, but it doesn't feel right. More likely, Junior is in the Hamptons, and it's not so easy to stalk me when I'm here, and Junior is there.

It's close to three when I arrive at Kane's place, our place, and this time, there is nothing waiting for me at the desk when I arrive. I wave to the guard, another familiar face, and head for the elevator when my weather app sends me an alert: *Hurricane season isn't over yet as Tropical Storm Beth charges toward the Long Island coastline, bringing torrential rains.*

Fuck. Rain. That's what he's waiting for and Beth? It's really called Beth? I step into the elevator and try to call Beth, but I have no signal. Impatient, I wait until I'm on our floor, and I dial again. Beth doesn't answer. I leave a voicemail. "Beth. You're there? All is well? We haven't talked since you got there, but I need you to have your security person call me. *Now.* It would be excellent if he could do that now." Fuck. I just made her panic. I decide not to speak another word. I'll just stop now.

I disconnect and hurry past our apartment security. The minute I'm inside the apartment, I call Kane. "Did you meet with Roger?"

"Not that now. Tropical storm Beth is coming. That means rain and murder, and it's Beth. That means something. I need the number to Beth's security person."

"I'm texting it to you now. I have to go into a meeting. I'll call you right after."

179

"Yes. Okay." I hang up and dial the security person, updating him as I start a pot of coffee. He's with Beth, and he places her on the line.

"Listen, it's probably nothing, but the rain, the blood, the storm named Beth. I just want you to be careful."

"I'm here. The guard is great. I feel pretty okay here."

"The guard is great? And you feel okay there? Okay. That's unexpected but good. And even better, you're getting your samples."

"I heard. You know this is saving the lab six figures. That's how much getting in this same equipment would have cost them. All and all, this worked out. I'm digging in the minute the samples arrive. Any leads?"

"I'm working on some things." It's not really much of an answer but it turns into chit chat that really isn't my thing, but I manage. The minute I hang up, my mind goes to Beth's family. Damn it. They could end up suicide victims. I dial Jay and make arrangements to protect them. I'm literally using an army of Kane's resources. I try not to think about what else he uses those resources for or how fucked up and contradictory it's all becoming. Then again, maybe helping me is like my marks on the back of our photo. He's redeeming himself. A good for a bad. He might need to do a lot of good. Why the hell doesn't that bother me more than it does? That's the reality here. I'm not as rattled by who and what Kane is as I vocalize. And he knows it.

With coffee and strawberries in hand, I head to Purgatory and sit down at my desk. I don't shut the door. I've always shut the door while in Purgatory, but not this one, not here. I'm not going to analyze why that is right now. The many layers to who I am with Kane Mendez are far too complicated and problematic. And good, but that's another topic, too. I open my bag and set the pig on top of the desk. I should have left it for evidence but that meant Thomas, and for reasons I still can't identify, I'm uncomfortable with that man. I'm actually uncomfortable with most people, but I deal with it. I just can't with him.

I stare at my board and repeat the data I know, looking for things that are similar and different between the two women. Mia had a boyfriend. Shelly didn't.

I dig through my paperwork to confirm. I'm correct. Shelly had no boyfriend. I also get irritated at Greg for not returning my calls. I dial him now. "Okay, asshole," I say to his voicemail. "Whatever is going on with you, this is it. I got you back your job. Come Monday, it's gone. Did I say asshole? I need you. I have something big going on." I hang up.

My phone rings, and lo and behold, it's Greg. "Thank you, asshole, for calling back. What the fuck?"

"I'm on a job. Private hire. It pays big. I'm not coming back. You should consider it. It's damn good pay."

"I'm not in this for the money."

"Right. Rich bitch and all. You can buy me a drink when I get back next week."

"Where are you?"

"Mexico. Heard a lot of shit about Kane Mendez down here. I'll fill you in."

Says a man who was sleeping with a Romano, when a Romano killed Kane's father, I think. "I don't need to hear about Kane. I know about Kane."

"I doubt it. I doubt it very seriously, or else you're not the person I know you to be."

"I'm not, Greg," I say before I can stop myself. It's out. It's that whole embrace who you are lecture of Kane's. It's gone to my head.

"Maybe you aren't. But then maybe I'm not who you thought I was either. Later, Lilah." He disconnects, and I sigh. He's getting himself in trouble. I feel it. Then again, so am I, or I wouldn't have run my mouth like that.

I text Houston: *Your guy is in. Mine is out.*

He replies with: *The mayor wants you fired.*

I reply with: *The mayor needs to eat a cookie and wax his bald head.*

He answers with: *In case you didn't see. He held the press conference. He told the city that Ralph's suicide was a tragic accident and the two murders were isolated and unrelated.*

My cellphone rings, and it's Murphy. I answer, "Hello, Director Murphy," all polite and official, like a sweet innocent girl or something.

"*Don't be stupid*? To the mayor, Lilah?"

"You can't hide from stupid. His press conference will be answered and not by me. But by the asshole I'm hunting who wants attention he didn't get. Saying nothing was better than stealing his thunder."

"He wants you fired."

That's all he's going to fucking say? "Okay," I reply. "Am I fired?"

"No, Agent Love, but if you make me come back to New York to save your ass, neither of us will enjoy my visit."

"If you come here, you can do your own dirty work rather than using Kane, because that's where this is headed, right?"

"I didn't know you needed Kane to do your dirty work."

"My dirty work?"

"Your dirty work is mine. If you don't get that, you will. Stop pissing me off. Now get to work." He hangs up. And this hang up shit continues and continues.

I return to my note cards and focus on the one for Detective Lori Williams

Redhead

Police detective

Boyfriend

Killed stepmom

Mom in a nursing home

Father dead

In my mind that bird and that man from those insurance commercials come to my mind: *What do all of these people have in common? Nothing. That's exactly right.*

I groan. The answer is not *nothing*. I shove a strawberry in my mouth and wash it down with coffee. I then pace, sit down, repeat. I look at the pig. I write down my name and Kane's name again. I write down the words "the Society." I set that card aside. I think that Beth being involved is what got me shoved down that rabbit hole. This is not the Society.

They'd do an assassination, clean and done. This is not clean and done. And Kane went to war with Pocher recently and won. I don't believe Pocher would cross him this fast or this directly. No. The Society is out.

I write down "Junior" and set that card aside. Again, Junior feels like someone from the Hamptons, someone far less sophisticated than Umbrella Man. I write down "Roger" and stare at the name before sliding my name next to his. This guy is someone who has watched one or both of us; perhaps, we've crossed paths. Perhaps he was a part of one of our cases in the past.

"Damn it," I murmur and dial Roger.

"Lilah. Or *Agent Love*. Interesting case. Melanie filled me in on the details."

Of course, she did. "What unsolved cases do you have that connect to these cases? What unsolved cases did we have that connects to these cases?"

"I can't think of any."

"Me either, but I feel like there's something we're forgetting, a connection, past or present."

"Maybe we should sit down and go through our old cases, and you can tell me what's leading you here."

Fuck.

Fuck.

Fuck.

"You go through your cases. If you see anything, send it to me."

"No to a meeting. Why Lilah? What's going on?"

"Murder, Roger. It's a little time consuming. Let me know."

I disconnect and stare at his name on the paper. He was my mentor. I wanted to please him, but there was a point, in the end, where we started butting heads. That constant push and pull of me questioning him and him questioning me made leaving easier. No. I'm lying to myself. Killing someone and fearing he'd know is what made leaving so damn easy.

My gaze lands on the pig Umbrella Man left me at the diner where Maria Mendez worked. He was bringing attention to Kane. Was he telling me, through Kane, that he knows who and what I really am? Was he telling me that we're the same? Are we both killers hiding in plain sight? Was this his way of telling me that I'm looking right at him? He's right in front of me. He's close. He's telling me that he knows me, and I know him. He's so damn close, and that's dangerous.

CHAPTER THIRTY-FOUR

Kane calls me about an hour into my Purgatory torture. "Everything handled?"

"Aside from the storm I can't shut down and despite knowing that's when he kills again, yes. It's all just peachy fucking keen."

"Are you going to tell me what happened with Roger or are we avoiding that topic?"

"I'm not avoiding anything including him. Yes, damn it, I saw him. He was far less intimidating than I remember."

"You're afraid of yourself, not him,"

"Are you my shrink now?"

"I was repeating what you said earlier but I'm anything you need me to be, Lilah Love."

"Now? Here?"

"Not yet. I'm taking care of that problem. And it's like your storm. I can't seem to shut it down. I'll be home as soon as I can."

We end the call and that word "home" lingers in my mind. The thing is, since my mother died, there's no place that feels like home, except here with Kane. My phone rings again, and this time, it's my brother. I let it ring and go to voicemail. I do actually listen to the voicemail, which is all about family and support and getting my ass to the party. I consider calling back to tell him a few things, but that would earn me a lecture that would exhaust me. I need to catch a killer, and that's my focus. I focus on pigs, umbrellas, and a monster. In doing so, at some point, time passes fairly rapidly and I end up in the center of the floor with papers everywhere, some of which are mini Hershey wrappers because, yes, Kane bought me chocolate. At present, I'm contemplating Murphy as the Umbrella Man, which tells you how desperate I am. I shut my eyes and will a real answer, that one in the back of my mind, to materialize. I open my eyes, and Kane is standing over me, and damn the man makes a suit look good. No wonder I give in to the sins of his dark world. Look at the man.

"Hi," I say.

"Hi, beautiful," he says, "I was glad to see you come home to work earlier, just like old times."

"You saw me because you were watching me."

"Yes, Lilah. I was watching you."

"Stalker."

"You can watch me, too. We have cameras."

"That you record *everything* on."

He catches my hand and pulls me to my feet. "We can watch that together."

"You're dirty."

"You like me dirty." He strokes hair away from my face and kisses me hard and fast. "How is it coming?"

"Like shit. He's close. He's someone I know, maybe we know."

"I'm gathering that considering that Mendez name today."

My cellphone rings, and I glance down at it on the floor to find my brother calling again. "Good lord. He's stalking me now."

"We need to go shower and get dressed." He takes my hand and leads me toward the door, stepping over papers. "I see you found the chocolate."

"We need another bag, and we're not donating to my father's campaign. He already has my mother's money."

We step into the bathroom, and he kisses my hand. "No donation." He catches the hem of my T-shirt. "Let me help you with that."

"Because you're so helpful." I push away from him. "I've got it."

"I'm not helpful?" He shrugs out of his jacket.

I toss my shirt and unhook my bra. His gaze rakes over me, hot and heavy, before he pulls me to him. "What do you need help with now, Lilah?"

"Nothing that requires clothing."

He catches a handful of my hair, and his mouth comes down on mine. From there, he doesn't disappoint. Our clothes come off, and I'm reminded of how easily this man can make me forget even the worst, most horrific crimes, if only for a short while, but that escape keeps me human. He's not going to make me a monster. He's going to keep me from becoming one. We end up with me on the sink and him inside me, and when it's over, he presses his cheek to mine and whispers, "I missed the hell out of you."

And for the first time since I've come back, I answer with what I really feel. "I missed you, too."

He pulls back and stares down at me, his expression unreadable and intense before he kisses me again and carries me to the shower. A long time later, I've indulged that part of me that is my mother's daughter—the part that loves pretty things. I'm in the bathroom finishing up in a pink form-fitting knee-length dress, my lips painted the same shade, my hair a shiny silky brown around my shoulders. Kane joins me in his tuxedo, looking all Latin Stallion, with that air of danger especially edgy tonight.

"God, woman," he says, pulling me close. "You look stunning."

"Thank you," I say, and it's not awkward. He means his words. He just changes me. "I'll certainly confuse a few people, fuck with some minds, you know?"

"And we know how much you love that." His cellphone rings, and he snakes it from his pocket, glancing at the number. His expression tightens, and he releases me to answer the line.

"What now?" he asks. "No. Fuck, no." He shifts to Spanish and gives me his back, walking out of the bathroom to the bedroom, where I pick up a few key lines like "Do I need to show him who the real fucking Mendez is?" That one gets me. I lean on the sink and squeeze my eyes shut, hating this is his world, our world, but I know Kane. I know he's forced into this. I know he can't just walk away.

When he stops speaking, I enter the bedroom to find him standing at the window, one hand on the wall, his gaze on the skyline that is alight with the city, but I know that's not what he sees. I know he's in his head. I need to be there, too.

I close the space between us and slip between him and the window. "I heard the part about the real Mendez."

His lashes lower, and he turns away, giving me his back again, but then he rotates to face me. "You know I do what I have to do. You know this."

"I'm not judging you, Kane. I told you. You can trust me."

"I fucking trust you, Lilah. We've had this conversation. It's not about trust. What you don't know can't hurt you."

"Okay, damn it. Forget all of that. You're about to explode right now. If that were me, I'd talk to you. I'd break the rules and talk to you. Talk to me."

"My uncle is missing, Lilah. His right hand man wants to kill everyone he can find to kill, to make this right."

"Oh fuck."

"Yes. Oh fuck."

"You have to take control."

"Do you understand what you just said to me?"

"Come on, Kane. You *are* your father's son. You are who they all wanted in his place. You can stop this."

"What I want is to let them all kill themselves, but you know why I can't?" He doesn't give me time to respond. "Because the Society stepped back from the cartel. I made peace with Romano, despite knowing he killed my father for that very reason. I made peace with every enemy my father created, of which there were many, for that reason. And the minute we're fighting amongst ourselves, the Society eats us alive."

"You already are in control, or you couldn't have made peace. Do what you have to do and don't hide it from me."

"You can't be FBI and be with me if I'm pulled deeper into this."

"You already are. We both know it." I step to him. "I'm not giving you permission to be a monster. I'm telling you that I will keep you in the middle. I'm not leaving again. You do what you need to do."

"Lilah, you don't know—"

"I know everything about you, even the things you don't want me to know. I'm not leaving."

He catches my head and kisses me. "Holy fuck, woman, I love you."

"I love you, too. Now what?"

"Now we go to the party and show the Society we're in control."

"But what about your problem?"

"It's contained, at least for the moment."

A few minutes later, we step outside to find rain falling, and in it, I swear I see blood. Death is coming at us from all directions.

CHAPTER THIRTY-FIVE

I shared a love for the Metropolitan Museum with my mother. Now, believing my father might have been involved in her death, even indirectly, I resent his fundraiser being held there. There is, however, another part of me that finds the pink dress and location such a part of her that it's necessary. Because she was necessary. She made herself matter. She was good. She was what I wish I could be and never can be, but Kane and I both need me to try at least a little right now.

We arrive at the event in a hired a car, and it's not long until we're inside a building of towering ceilings, amazing sculptures, and clusters of tuxedos and sparkling dresses. Of course, there are also banners and balloons that all say Love for Governor. There are also waiters with finger foods roaming the room, the kind of nasty shit no one really wants. "Why can't they just give us chocolate and champagne?" I ask.

Kane catches a waiter with a tray of the latter. I accept a glass. "One of the two," he says. "Better than nothing."

"Do you know what I want?"

"To be the hell out of here?"

"Aside from that. I want to go see the dinosaurs. We should sneak out."

"Let's show our faces and then we'll find the dinosaurs." He offers me his arm, and we start the torturous process of greeting people who are all giddy over my father. "You must be so proud!" one woman says. "He'll be incredible!" another says.

"Shoot me and bury me beside my mother," I murmur.

"Can't do that," Kane says. "You aren't leaving me, remember?"

I'd reply but Houston steps in front of us.

"Guess who?" he says, planting himself in front of me and then immediately glancing at Kane. "Kane Mendez." He offers Kane his hand. "Chief Houston. I'm the new kid on the block who was forced to come tonight."

Kane stares at him. That's all. Just stares. He doesn't reach for his hand. He's so damn cold; it's really quite an impressively icy showing. Houston bristles awkwardly, and I barely contain a laugh but I put him out of his misery.

"He works for Murphy," I tell Kane. "He might be okay. I haven't decided yet."

Houston gives me a "what the fuck" look. "Was that supposed to help my case?" He meets Kane's stare and lowers his voice. "I'm a friend, and you need friends like me."

"I don't have friends," Kane says. "What do you need from me?"

"Ouch." He drops his hand and tugs at the lapels of his tux. "And I thought this thing was torture. I'll try another time." He glances at me. "You see the press conference?"

"Your text was enough. He wrote Detective Williams' death wish. He'll regret it. Unfortunately, she won't. She'll be dead."

His expression tightens. "I know. I hate this shit and then they made me come to this."

"Who made you?" Kane asks.

"Murphy. He said Lilah might need me."

"I didn't tell Murphy I'd be here," I snap.

"Don't give him too much magical power," Houston says. "It's in the promo material for tonight. The future Governor Love with his son and daughter by his side."

"Why would she need you?" Kane asks, still on the topic of Murphy sending Houston to the party.

"I think it's more about me earning acceptance," Houston says. "He doesn't want me to seem like *their* enemy."

I read between the lines considering "he" is Murphy. He means Pocher and his Society.

"High alert, baby, is all I can say to you, boy" he says. "High alert. Hoping we don't find Williams tonight in all the wrong ways. Anyway, let me go pretend I like these people and get out of here." He fades into the crowd.

I step in front of Kane. "You don't like him."

"Aside from the fact that he called us both *baby,* I don't like anyone in this room, but you. And this game Director Murphy is playing is not sitting well."

"About that and him—"

"There she is." My brother's voice is followed by his hands on my shoulders and him turning me to face him. "I knew you'd make it."

"Andrew. You're touching me."

"You're my sister," he says, his blue eyes twinkling with mischief, because he knows I hate when anyone touches me, well, except for Kane. "I can touch you."

"When we were ten, and even then, a hug was generally followed by a punch. I punch harder now." Andrew's gaze lifts over my shoulder to Kane, a crackle of tension in the air. He invited Kane, but just two weeks ago, he and Rich worked hard to try to take Kane down, to prove him a criminal.

I twist around to stand with them on either side of me. "You both asked for this tonight."

Andrew runs a hand through his blond hair and curses. "It's awkward right? But we'll get by it." He offers Kane his hand. "Truce."

Kane doesn't even think about lifting his hand. "I got her here," Kane says. "That's all the truce you get."

"Jesus," I murmur. "Okay. Well. Now what, you two?"

"For me and Kane," Andrew says , "apparently there will be no hand shaking. For you and me, Dad wants us with him when he speaks in about fifteen minutes," Andrew says, but he's still looking at Kane. "I love her, man. We both know you're into some shit, but I know you protect her, too. I've been thinking about that shit. You know that has value. And you're why she's here—at this party and here, in New York. That's all." He looks at me. "We'll call for you over the intercom." He disappears into the crowd.

I step in front of Kane again and just look at him. "What do you want me to say, Lilah?"

"Nothing. I get it. All of it."

He downs his champagne and sets his glass on a passing waiter's tray before catching my hip and walking me closer. "You want me to make peace with him."

"No."

His hands come down on my arms. "I will. For you. *Anything* for you."

My cold, bitter heart warms for this man.

"Lilah Love and Kane Mendez."

At the sound of Pocher's voice, my heart goes cold again. I grind my teeth. Kane pulls me around, his arm around me, his hand settling at my hip possessively. Pocher steps directly in front of us, a tall, thin man with salt and pepper hair. His tuxedo is expensive, but then he's a billionaire political machine, so why wouldn't it be?

"Pocher," Kane greets.

Pocher gives me a once over. "As I said, you remind me of your mother."

It's not a compliment. It's a threat. My mother is dead, and I believe that's because she got in his way. "And you, I hear," I say, "resemble your bother. How is he after his return from that nasty cartel? Thank God, Kane was able to help you get him back."

Kane's fingers flex on my hip, and it's not a warning, it's approval. "Yes," Kane joins in. "How is he? Is he *safe* now?"

And that, my friends, is a subtle, but lethal threat from Kane Mendez delivered with a whip of confidence that bites.

Pocher responds instantly. His gaze jerks to Kane's, and he lowers his voice. "I made a deal. I'm keeping the deal. Leave my brother out of this." There is something akin to desperation in his voice. He's afraid of Kane, really damn afraid. What the hell did Kane have done to his brother? "You could have let him keep his finger."

"Oh fuck," I murmur.

"Yes, Agent Love. Oh, fuck."

"I saved him," Kane says. "I had nothing to do with what the men who kidnapped him did to him. And saving him didn't come without a price. I had to make deals. I had to call in favors.]I had to spend money and shed blood. This caused me the kind of trouble that will come back to you if you come back at Lilah."

"Lilah is safe." He looks at me. "I do things for the greater good. Your father in office is for the greater good. You can help. I suggest you do." He looks at Kane. "We're powerful, Kane Mendez. Don't underestimate us." His attention flicks to me again. "Five minutes until the announcements. Be at the front of the room." He leaves, but the threat he just issued stays right here with us.

CHAPTER THIRTY-SIX

Kane and I rotate to each other. "They took his finger?" I ask. "I saw him after he returned. I didn't even notice."

"They did." His lips quirk. "And as to that, at least they didn't kill him."

It's a reference to my father telling me at least Pocher didn't kill me. He just had me raped. "You knew."

"I told you, Lilah. I know what he did to you now, and he will pay."

The punch between us with those words is hard and intense. And it's all there. My rape. Me killing that man. Him burying the body. Our time apart. "Kane—"

"I will never let you down again, Lilah, and he knows that now. My only regret is that it wasn't *his* finger, but now he gets to wonder what I might take from him."

If Kane Mendez said that about me, even I would be scared. There are things I want to say to him, so many things, but not here. "Are you worried about his threat?"

"No. And me being here tonight by your side tells him that. I told you. I build allies. We both agreed tonight that I'm not letting that fall apart." He takes my hand. "Let's move to the front and try to get your reunion with your father over with."

We weave through the crowd, and as we reach the front of the room, I spy my father in conversation with someone I do not expect. He's in deep conversation with Roger.

"Is that expected?" Kane asks.

"No. No, I didn't even know he'd be here."

"Murphy again?"

"If it's Murphy," I glance up at him, "we might have to make it without my badge."

"Or we do it without Murphy."

"Or that."

I glance toward Roger again, and this time, he catches us in his line of sight, motioning us forward.

Kane repositions us and places himself directly in front of Roger. I don't miss that move. I doubt Roger does either. "There she is," Roger greets. "Looking like your mother indeed. I was just telling your father what an honor it was to work with you." His gaze shifts to Kane. "The man and the mystery right here in front of me."

My father and I look at each other. He looks good, younger than his fifty-seven years, his blond hair more gray now. Ironically, he's the one Andrew got his blond hair from. My mother was a brunette. "Hug your father," he orders softly. "People are watching."

"And I should do what people expect?"

"Yes, Lilah. You should."

My jaw sets. "I don't think I will."

"Why come if you're not going to show support?" He moves toward me, and I let him hug me, but in my mind, all I hear is "at least they didn't kill you."

He releases me and flicks a look at Kane then back to me. "I know you love him. I've spoken with Pocher. There is strength in us all coming together. Tonight is good. I need you on stage by my side."

"I'll be right there," I say, still digesting the fact that he just basically told me that he thinks this truce between us and the Society means that Kane is now an ally. I think of Murphy's agenda. They all want Kane, and they're all going through me to get to him.

I turn to Kane and Roger. Roger is trying to hold a conversation. That doesn't really work with Kane, but in this moment, I decide Roger is here to try to get a read on Kane, to try to find a weakness beyond me. Which could mean he's with Pocher which would explain my change of heart with him that dates back to before I left. It could even be about his intrigue for a man like Kane, or the fact that Kane is suing the department, but whatever the case, I don't like it. It pisses me off. I close the space between me and the two men, closing my hand down on Kane's arm, stepping close to him. "I didn't know you were coming tonight, Roger," I say. "How did that happen?"

"The entire building is filled with law enforcement. Your father is one of us, former police chief and all. I was going to mention it today, but we lost each other."

"You didn't even mention it on the phone."

"Yes, well, you got me all absorbed in this case of yours. As for old cases that might link to these new ones, I might have a few we can look at."

"May I have your attention!" It's my brother at the podium. "We're about to get started."

"Can I speak to you?" I ask, turning to Kane.

He nods, and I take his hand, guiding him toward a gap in the crowd and then toward the side of the stage. "You know this is all about you, right? They want you under their thumb."

"Do they?"

"You knew coming into this?"

"Of course, I knew. I do nothing without intent. You knew, too."

He's right. Ultimately, I did, but I keep secretly yearning for everything I think about my father to be all wrong. It's like my fear of looking into Roger's eyes. It's distracting. And I have that fear with my father. I'm not afraid he'll see me. I'm afraid I'll see him.

A woman steps to my side. "We need you."

"Of course you do." I wave her off. "The minute I step off that stage, we leave."

Kane arches a brow. "No dinosaurs?"

"I believe I've had enough dinosaurs tonight."

"Good point," he says. "I'll be right here waiting on you, beautiful." He leans in close, and whispers. "And you are beautiful tonight, Lilah."

I melt a little. This man is the only person on planet earth that can make me melt like a girl. I like it. I like it a lot. Somehow, that little comment makes my walk to the stage shorter, the face to face with Mayor Ellison that follows, almost palpable. "Agent Love. I didn't know you were your father's daughter. It explains a lot."

"I don't know what that means, and frankly, I don't care." I try to step around him.

He blocks me. "I had to do it. You convinced me that the only win was the one that made the city feel safer."

"They won't feel safer when Umbrella Man makes you look stupid."

Andrew steps to our sides, and I twist away from the mayor. Soon, I'm on the stage as my father talks, and if I didn't know he was a bastard, I'd vote for him. Okay, I wouldn't. I don't vote. I've seen too much. I know they all suck. My gaze shifts often to Kane and his is always on me until a phone call grabs his attention. It's not a good call either. He walks away. Kane wouldn't walk away with me on stage unless privacy was critical. Time begins to pass brutally slow. Finally, the speech winds down, and my father says we have a very special American flag cake tonight made by the Sweet Kings, just for us. A huge draped display is rolled out and drums roll, literally. Talk about overkill.

The drape is pulled, and I'm anticipating at least a piece of cake to remember this night by when gasps fill the room. There is no cake. It's a very large dead pig dripping blood.

Chaos erupts, and Andrew turns to me. "What the hell?" My father steps to our circle.

"It's a gift to the mayor from the killer we're hunting," I say. "I told him not to speak today. Get everyone out of here. He likes poison."

Andrew takes control of the stage, and the microphone, speaking to the crowd while I talk to security. We get the guests moving to the doors, and finally, I make my way to the side of the stage to have Kane lift me from the top. He takes my hand and walks me away from the crowd, tension radiating off of him. That call was trouble. There's more going on than a pig at a party. He pulls me around a corner and into a hallway.

"I need to go to Texas," he says. "Now. That problem exploded."

"Now?"

"Now. Come with me. Get away from this."

"You know I can't do that. I can't leave when someone could end up dead."

"We'll be back by late tomorrow."

"No. I can't. I need to get back in there."

He cuts his stare, clearly battling with his need to leave before he fixes me in a turbulent stare. "Then I'm having Jay stay the night in the apartment with you." Jay steps around the corner. "He's your shadow."

"I don't need Jay to stay with me."

He cups my face. "You will do this for me, woman. I can't deal with this and worry about you."

His voice vibrates with those words. Kane's voice doesn't vibrate. He's on edge. This problem is bad, maybe even worse than I know. "Yes. Yes, okay." I ease back to look at him, that emotion that only he stirs in me welling in my chest. "No one kills you but me. You understand?"

"I'll be back. You're here." He kisses me, deep and passionate, and then he leaves me with Jay, a dead pig, and a bunch of politicians.

CHAPTER THIRTY-SEVEN

"What can I do now?" Jay asks.

"Look for the sick bastard," I say. "He's here, watching the show. And look for Detective Williams. She's next."

He nods and heads back into the main party as I do the same. I'm greeted by Andrew and Houston. "We got your father, the mayor, and Pocher out of here," Houston says. Apparently, my father demanded it. "I'm calling in a forensics team now that we have the place clear."

A man who actually knows his job, thank you, Lord.

"What is this, Lilah?" Andrew asks.

"I told you what this is, and I warned Mayor Ellison not to taunt this guy." I consider sharing details and decide I have no choice. "He picks targets and goes after their loved ones first. He makes them commit suicide to save the real victims, but he kills them anyway. He's fixated on me. I think that I'm just part of the game, not a victim, but you need to be careful and make sure dad's people are on high alert."

"I really hate that this is your job," Andrew says. "Can you quit already? I mean you and Kane are both rich. Just quit." He's serious. He's frazzled, and my bother isn't one to get frazzled, but he's also the human side of this family and thank God for him.

I grab his arm. "I'm good, okay? I promise. I'm not a delicate flower."

"But you bleed, Lilah."

"Not anytime soon. I'm too much of a bitch. You told me so more than once. Go make sure dad's safe. And stay in the Hamptons until this is over."

"Come with me."

"I can't do that. Go, Andrew."

He scrubs his jaw. "I need to tell you that dad took Roger with him. The mayor wanted his input."

I don't even blink. "Good." I think. "Every pain in my ass but you are now in one place."

He laughs. "You mean that don't you?"

"Oh, hell yeah, I mean that. Go be with them and then you'll all be in one place."

"Fine. I'm going. Call me when you get home."

"Don't count on it." I motion him away. "Go. Leave. Now."

"Call me, you pain in my ass."

"No." He scowls and kisses my temple before he leaves.

I turn my attention to Houston, and he says, "I got this, Lilah. You go do whatever profilers do." "We're going to lock this place down and require special gear."

"I need to walk the scene."

"Hell no. We have no dead body this time. We aren't taking the risk of extra personnel, you included, walking around the place."

"We're walking around it now."

"Which is stupid. That is the word of the day, right?"

"Okay, but the cameras and—"

"I got it all," he promises. "Cameras, witnesses, prints, you name it. Go do the part that might actually catch this guy."

"You might be decent at your job."

"I'll tell you a secret: Murphy doesn't hire assholes and bitches who can't get the job done. I'm gone now to do my job. You be gone, too, out of the building."

"I said you *might* be good at your job. That's not good enough, and this is my jurisdiction now. I'm not going anywhere. Get me suited up."

He scowls the way Andrew had—I do that to people—but I get what I want. I take over the scene, and I suit up. I'm on the hunt for a killer who I intend to kill before he kills again. Kane is on his way to Texas where I believe he intends to kill someone, too. We are both the perfect couple and a perfect nightmare.

***

The pig tells a story, and it's not about the three little piggies that went to market. It's about an asshole who kills animals and women. Maybe he'd even kill children. I want him dead. I don't even pretend otherwise. If Umbrella Man's messages tell a story, it's not the one he wants it to tell. It's about his own death.

With Kane gone, but on my mind, and the dead pig taunting me like it's a killer, the investigation proves slow going and tedious. Samples are collected. Interviews are done. Cameras were knocked out despite high security. No one seems to know where the cake went, but it was seen here at the museum, which at least tells us the investigation starts here, not at the cake shop. One worker even took a photo. No one has any idea how the pig could have been snuck in, but I do. This is someone in law enforcement. The dramatics of the pigs still might be what does Umbrella Man in. Any sample of soil or a twig could tell us where he went to get the pigs he's slaughtered.

It's hours later and after midnight when I finally slide into the back seat of the hired car where I find Jay waiting for me, and a driver behind the wheel. "I'm done. We can leave."

Jay motions to the driver, and we start moving. "Anything from Kane?" I ask.

"Kane doesn't report to you or me. You don't know as much as I thought you did or you wouldn't ask me that."

"And so we wait."

"Because you won't call him."

"I'm not going to distract him and get him killed."

"I reverse my decision," he declares. "You know more than I thought you knew."

I don't reply with a normal "fuck you" or some other remark. Exhaustion has taken hold. I need to sleep. I need to hear from Kane. I grab my phone and open a text message. I don't know what to type, and no matter what I choose, I could still distract him. I slide my phone back into my purse.

A few minutes later, Jay follows me into the apartment. "There's a spare bedroom off the kitchen or downstairs," I say. "Use one."

"I need to be in the main room by the door."

"If you sleep on my fancy couch, I'll shoot you. Your decision."

"Floor it is."

"And don't eat my ice cream."

"Or you'll shoot me."

"Exactly. Now you're learning. I'm going to bed." I head toward the stairs.

"I guess pink doesn't make you less of a bitch," he calls after me.

I ignore him, and it's not long before I'm laying in bed, the scent of Kane all around me, but he hasn't called. I'm thinking about him, not the killer. Kane is strong. He's smart. He doesn't die easily, but this trip is not a normal trip. I told him to do what he had to do. I told him I'd accept what he had to become. I gave him a license to kill, but those who kill can be killed.

CHAPTER THIRTY-EIGHT

I wake to my cellphone ringing, but, this time, it's also to sunshine and an empty bed. My phone is laying on my chest. I grab it and answer without looking at the number. "Kane?"

"The press is a nightmare." It's Houston, and I grimace and throw away the blankets. "They're all over me, the station, and yes, we made the headlines," he continues. "There's a picture of the pig. And it gets worse. One headline reads '*Serial Killer in New York City.*'"

"Of course it does," I say, swinging my legs over the side of the bed. "This is what he wants, and after last night, what we all should have expected."

"What the mayor and the DA want is my blood. I'd ask you to come in, but you'll get us both fired. You with them scares me."

"Me with them is what they deserve, but it's not what I deserve. I'm not going. I'm working the case."

"Can you catch him already?"

I hang up. Asshole. Like I'm not trying, but he's right; I need to catch the killer already. I glance at the clock and read the ten am hour. Kane's been gone twelve hours, and it's twelve hours of silence. "Damn it," I murmur, and this part of living with Kane isn't going to be easy. It was much easier when we pretended I didn't know what was going on when we both pretended these trips were just straight-up business. He's alive or Jay would have told me. Or maybe he wouldn't.

Damn it again, I need to work and stay busy. I hurry into the bathroom and take a quick shower. It's close to eleven when I'm finally dressed in jeans, a black tank top, and sneakers. My hair is even dry. I'm going to be brilliant today. I did only put mascara on one eye at one point, but I fixed it.

That's all that really matters. And my socks don't match, but no one will know, except fucking Kane if he would just come home. I head downstairs and find Jay asleep on the floor. "Move to the bed," I call out. "I'm awake and without coffee, which means I'm ready to shoot anyone who walks in the door. I'll also enjoy shooting whoever comes in the door." I start a pot of coffee. My cellphone rings, and it's my brother.

"You okay?"

I frown. "What the fuck, Andrew. Am I okay? Of course, I'm fucking okay. Are *you*?"

"No, I'm not okay. I spent hours with dad, the mayor, and Roger, hearing about how creepy this case is you're working."

"No Pocher?"

"He doesn't associate with us lower beings except in public."

"Ah well none of those lower beings talking about my case know everything. It's much worse than they think."

"And that helps me feel better how?"

I sit down at the island and listen to my coffee brewing. It's a sweet sound. "I'm sorry. Did mom give birth to me to make you feel better because no one gave me those instructions?"

"You don't follow instructions."

"True." I sigh. "Look, Andrew. This is what I do, and Kane keeps me and him surrounded by security. One of which is asleep on my floor right now."

"What the hell did you do to him?"

"Get up, Jay! Go to the bed," I call out and then to Andrew, "I beat him. He deserved it. Then I made him sleep on my living room floor." I change the subject. "As for your little trio of plotters. I claimed jurisdiction on this case. It's federal now. The mayor, our daddy dearest, and Roger have no say."

"Why exactly did you do that?"

"Because this is personal. This guy used my boss, an FBI Director, to get to me. He wanted me. He got me. We're playing a game. I always win at games. You know this."

"This isn't Monopoly."

"But I always won, right?"

There's a call on his radio, and I hear the words "Police Chief."

"I have to go. Be careful. The mayor really hates you. I, on the other hand, love you, Lilah."

He doesn't wait for my reply. Love stuff gets awkward for the Love family. Perhaps the name predisposed us to that.

Jay drags himself to the kitchen. "Kane wanted you to call him when you woke up."

I have a good poker face, I do; I can have a killer hold a gun on me and never blink, but I know relief is washing over my expression like I'm a kid standing under Niagara Falls right now. I give a nod, fill a cup of coffee and sweeten it, before heading back upstairs where I can speak in private. The minute I'm in Purgatory at my desk, I dial Kane.

"Morning, beautiful."

I breathe out, just the sound of his voice is pure relief. "You should have fucking called sooner, Kane Mendez. Really. What the fuck?"

He gives a low laugh. "Worried?"

"Yes. I'm fucking worried. I was worried last night. I'm worried now."

"I had things to take care of when I arrived. You know that."

"And?"

"I'll tell you in person."

"Give me something."

"The problem is contained."

"And you are?"

"Not my uncle."

"That's almost unexpected."

"You underestimate me."

"Never," I assure him.

"What's happening there?"

"You know what matters. Another dead pig. An asshole father. The press going crazy. That sums up the key points."

"Any leads?"

"Not a one."

Someone says something to him in Spanish. "I need to go. I'm going to be back tonight, and Lilah, it's good to have you worry about me." He hangs up.

I scowl at the phone. "You're an asshole, Kane. Giving me a reason to worry sucks." I toss it down and get to work. I need to relook at everything fresh, except having Jay in the house feels weird. About an hour into my work, I head downstairs and find him on the couch, watching sports.

He stands up. There's a bag of Cheetos in front of him. "We going somewhere?"

"You ate my damn Cheetos?"

"I can't shoot someone if I'm weak."

He's got a point. We order pizza, and when it arrives, I stack a plate and head back to Purgatory. That's when Houston calls again. "They're talking about city curfews and shit like that."

"That's ridiculous. This guy isn't picking random people up."

"I think you better come down here."

"And this is just what he wanted. Us fighting over city curfews while he watches and laughs."

"Be careful. There's a mess of press. You need to approach on foot through the west entrance."

We disconnect, I pack up my field bag and toss in a foldable rain jacket in case the storm opens up on us. Once I'm downstairs, I motion to Jay. "I have to go to the station, and I hope you've showered." I eye his shirt that he's had on for a full two days now. "I don't like stinky people."

"Of course I showered; I just have no clothes to change into."

"Go change while I'm at the station. Please. And people say I don't say please, but they lie."

We head for the door. "I'm walking. The press has mobbed the station, and it's close. Any vehicle will just get trapped."

"It's raining," he informs me as we step into the elevator. "It started about thirty minutes ago, and it's not supposed to let up for the entire weekend."

He's right. We step to the building door and find that rain waiting outside, but there's more than rain waiting. This is the night. I feel it in my gut. This is when the Umbrella Man kills again.

CHAPTER THIRTY-NINE

I pull on my rain jacket and turn to Jay, considering him a moment before we exit the apartment building. "This is the night."

"He'll strike again?"

"Yes, and if you're with me, it's going to affect what he does next."

"I'm not leaving you," he snaps. "Kane will fucking kill me."

"I'm not stupid enough not to want backup with this guy on the loose, but we're stronger if he thinks I am. I need him to think you walked away. He's not going to strike on a daytime walk to the police station. Go fucking shower. Meet me there. I'll communicate. I won't leave without you at my back."

"I'm not letting you go alone. What part of Kane will kill me do you not understand?"

I don't like the way he's painting Kane. "Stop fucking saying that. Kane isn't going to kill you."

"I don't know if you know him or not. One minute I think you do, the next I don't. This is you, Lilah. This is the only fucking person he cares about. If I leave you exposed, he will—"

"If you say what you're about to say, *I'll* fucking kill you. If you walk out of this door and he sees you, I will kill you. Don't you get it? If he kills Williams in private, I can't save her. If he tries to kill her in front of me, I have a chance to save her. I'm walking out of this door, and I swear to God, if you risk this woman's life, it will be your last stupid mistake."

I walk out of the door, and damn it, it's really coming down. I could go back to the doorman for an umbrella, but I have a particular aversion to those things right now, especially since Umbrella Man could be under one of the dozens on the sidewalks I'm now walking. I grab my phone and dial the medical examiner. It's a quick transfer to Melanie's voicemail. Of course, it's Saturday. I dial Beth.

"Agent fucking Love. I like this security guard."

"What happened to the FBI agent?"

"A fling with an asshole. Don't get me started."

"Yeah, about that. You said," I dodge an umbrella that almost takes my eye out, "a few weeks back, you said you were destined to be alone because of the dead body habit."

"Dead body habit? I'm a medical examiner, Lilah."

"Whatever."

"And we lasted like ten days. I wouldn't say that redefines that statement."

"How did you meet him?"

"At a crime scene."

"What crime scene?"

"Gang initiation murder. He's on a gang task force."

It makes sense. That would be an FBI operation. "Okay."

"Why?"

"Let's just change subjects. I'm on a tight schedule here. I'm about two blocks from a press zoo at the station. Do we have any word on what the toxin is?"

"No. I talked to Melanie last night and we've got a list of options, but this is a tough call to make."

"What do I do if I encounter someone dying from this shit again? Is there an antidote?"

"We don't know what we're dealing with, which makes that an impossible quest."

"Right. An impossible quest."

I round the corner to bring the zoo into view. "Try to come up with a better solution in the next few hours. I'm on a clock."

We disconnect and I cut around the building to the side door that has a barricade and a few uniformed officers in place. I flash my badge and head inside the door only to run smack into Moser. Again. "Why are you here?"

"I still have cases that people here need input on." He steps up to me. Close. Really close and I don't back away. "If I get fired, Lilah Love, you will feel the pain."

"You're about to feel the pain of my knee, asshole." I lift it and he steps back.

"Fuck you, Lilah." He walks around me and out of the building.

I wish Umbrella Man liked men, I think as I walk up the stairs and make my way to Houston's office. Of course, that's a nasty thought, but I'd say it out loud. I find Houston at his desk looking frazzled. "They're doing it. They're imposing a curfew. I'm having to call in an overtime crew."

"When is he announcing it?"

"A press conference in an hour."

"Give me fifteen minutes, and you owe me for this one," I say, exiting the office and finding an empty space, that I'd noticed on my last visit. I shut the door and call my father.

"Lilah," he says. "What the hell was that last night?"

"I thought Roger would explain."

"He says he's on the outside of this one. He suggested caution to Mayor Ellison."

"Mayor Ellison ignored me and held that press conference. He caused this. Is Pocher with you?"

"Yes. Why?"

"I need to talk to him," I say.

"I'm not letting you talk to my biggest asset."

"If you want to get elected, I suggest you put him on."

I hear a voice and then my father's grunt before Pocher greets me. "Agent Love."

"I assume you back Mayor Ellison based on party and his presence last night."

"You assume correctly."

"You want Mayor Ellison to hold his position and my father to claim the Governor's spot. Right now, Mayor Ellison is working to end his career, and his close proximity to my father will take him down as well."

"What are you recommending, Agent?"

"That you leash that loser and tell him that this is an FBI operation. If I have to seize his control, I will, even in the press, which is a fucked-up situation. There will be no curfew. That only gives this guy more of a high. He will feel in control. And he doesn't pluck random people off the street. This is a long, calculated process."

"What do you want Mayor Ellison to do?"

"No press conference. Issue a statement, that Chief Houston will write, which will say to the public that there is no reason for mass hysteria. We have no reason to believe there is a threat to the mass population. There are a few people involved in a calculated crime that the press has blown out of proportion."

"I'll make it happen."

"That's what I need to hear." I start to hang up.

"Agent Love."

"What?" I snap.

"We make a good team."

I could reply, but he's goading me. I don't take the bait. I hang up and return to Houston's office. "The curfew and press conference are off."

He stands ups. "How the hell did you make that happen?"

"I'm the magic bitch. You're writing a statement to the press about a confined set of crimes, no threat to the mass population, and the press sucks and lies. The mayor will issue that statement. While you do that, I'm going back to Detective Williams' place just to be sure he hasn't been back there."

I exit his office and text Jay: *Are you here?*

Damn straight I'm here, he replies.

I reply with: *I'm exiting from the west door, destination Detective Williams' place.*

Because why wouldn't we taunt the killer? he asks.

That's the plan. I want him to know I'm waiting for him. One read I have on him is that when challenged, he will respond. I'm going to make sure tonight is the night and it's his final night.

CHAPTER FORTY

Houston's on the phone to me before I ever leave the building. "I'm calling in that lead detective I suggested. One of the girls found a pig farm in Syracuse that's missing three pigs. I'm sending him out there."

"Which girl?" I ask, stepping out of the building.

"Lily."

"I need Lily's call records."

"Why?"

"I haven't had Starbucks today. I don't answer 'why' questions without Starbucks."

"Fuck, Lilah, can you tell me where your head is?"

"I don't trust anyone. I've told you this." I hang up and walk into a Starbucks, texting Jay again as I do: *Anything new from the people monitoring Lily?*

Nothing, he says.

I hate that word "nothing." It's as sucky as "I don't know."

Just for that, I type: *I bet you wish you could come out from the shadows where you're stalking me and have Starbucks.*

He replies with: *I prefer tequila. It's a Mexican thing.*

I reply with: *White girls drink tequila, too.*

His reply is one word: *Badly.*

I grimace and call an Uber, ordering a coffee while waiting for my ride. "Can I get a shot of tequila in that?"

The girl at the register gives me a blank stare. Holy fuck, can no one take a joke anymore? "Never mind. Just give me whipped cream and a Xanax."

She stares again.

"Whipped cream," I say, and decide I'm being punished for not using the app.

My coffee in hand, my Uber is slowly coming and with good reason. The rain is pounding down on us and the streets are far less crowded than they would be on any other

Saturday. By the time I pull up to Williams' place, it's somehow late afternoon. My cup is empty, and the caffeine has added to my agitation. I'm daring him to kill Williams by coming here. What I need to do is find her before he gets the chance.

Of course, I think, my hand on my weapon as I walk up the stairs, he could be here, she could be here, and that solves that. I reach the top of the stairs and find the door properly secured. I open it and enter, drawing my weapon as I walk the place. It's empty. It's as anticlimactic as meeting up with Roger again. Roger, I think, shoving my weapon in my holster. We solved a lot of damn cases together, and the clock really is ticking. I can't let my insecurities get in the way of my job.

I dial Roger. "Lilah, I'm surprised to hear from you. So much so that I was going to ask if there was something that happened between us that I didn't realize."

Obviously, I've made my discomfort apparent. I skip over that topic and get to the work at hand. "Can you meet and talk about this case?"

"You finally decided the old man can help?"

"Can you meet?" I press, not about to respond to that kind of bullshit he's trying to stir up.

"I'm on Long Island. I came up with the mayor last night and stayed over with my sister to catch up. I could be there around six. At the station?"

"It's a press madhouse." I decide being back in the area of the crime scenes might help me. "There's a diner across from the area where both murders took place. Let's meet there." I give him directions and end the call. Six. That's late. It might be too late to save Williams. I look around the apartment and start walking it again, looking for a trigger that tells me everything I need to know to catch this asshole.

***

Hours at Williams' place delivers a few items to follow up on that I call into Tic Tac, but nothing that feels big. I arrive at the diner I'd visited the night of the murders to find

Donna and I are the only ones here again. She waves when I arrive. "Pumpkin Latte?"

"What the fuck. Bring it on."

She laughs, and soon, I'm at a booth with coffee and lots of whipped cream. "Got my strawberry pie?"

"How the hell would I know you'd really be back?"

"Like you'd get it for me if you had."

The door opens and Roger enters, brushing rainwater from his jacket. "Lilah," he greets, waving and heading my way. He starts to cough. That cough gets to me. It stirs something inside me that I can't quite identify and I try to figure out when that started and why. Did he always cough like that? There is so much shit in between when I started with him and now.

He pauses by the booth and takes off his jacket, neatly folding it and draping it over the seat, before he sits down across from me, motioning to Donna. "Plain coffee."

Good luck with that, I think.

Roger moves his silverware to the side with one of his precise movements. He's a calculated man. Every I is dotted. Every box checked. He taught me to detail every crime scene with precision. I don't dispute, or lack appreciation for what the man did for my career.

"What's going on, Lilah?" he asks, studying me with those crystal blue eyes that I refuse to let intimidate me. If he wants to see a killer, see a killer, and fuck you, Roger.

Donna sets a pot down for Roger. I eye her. "He gets it without begging?"

"I already like him better than you."

"Bitch."

She grins and leaves.

Roger arches a brow at me. "We're old friends," I say. "Anyway, what's going on? Whoever this is, is targeting either me or you or both. He used you to get me here. He left your brand of cigarettes at the first crime scene. He's left me very personal messages."

"Then it's about you."

"Or me as your protégé."

"What kind of messages?" he queries.

"A link to Kane. A connection to a friend."

"You," he says, with certainty. "This is about you. Using me is still about you."

"The cigarettes disappeared from evidence. He's either law enforcement or using someone in law enforcement to do his dirty work."

"How would he use someone in law enforcement?"

I go through the entire case with him, and we go through cup after cup of coffee, throwing out ideas, talking about the details. I take pages of notes. We don't find the answers, but one thing about Roger is that he stimulates my mind. And thank fuck, he hasn't been coughing. I don't know how that's possible, but thank fuck anyway.

"What about Houston?" he asks. "He's the right age, in a position of power, and showed up right when this started. Where did he come from?"

My mind goes to his file. "LA. He worked with my boss in the past."

"Then he could have watched your work there."

He's right. He could have. Damn it, I trust Houston because of Murphy's placement, but why? I barely trust Murphy, and Kane doesn't trust Murphy at all. That just makes me trust Murphy even less. "I need to get to my desk and put all my notes to work." And pray Detective Williams survives the night. "Are you staying or going?"

"I think I'll order a bite to eat and think about this all a bit more."

"I'm going to walk and think."

"You sure that's safe?"

"I'm not just a profiler, Roger. I'm a field agent."

"Take an Uber, Lilah. It's raining."

I toss money on the table and slip into my rain jacket. "And Detective Williams might be on the street waiting for me to save her. I'm walking."

"If you invite him to come at you, he will."

I don't hesitate. "And I'll kill him with a big smile on my face." I text Jay that I'm coming out and wave to Donna before exiting the diner, pulling my hood up as the rain plummets me.

I stare across the street at Mia's apartment, and my gut twists. He's here. I know it. He's waiting for me. I came here for a reason. This is where it's going to happen. The alley. I call Jay. "I'm going to the alley. Stay back unless I call out for you." I hang up.

Hurrying across the street, I reach for my flashlight but don't turn it on. I pull my weapon and walk the two deserted blocks to the alley. I huff out a breath and step into the opening turning on my flashlight and aiming my weapon. Nothing. There is no one there. My heart is thundering. Fuck. I'm wrong. He's not here. Of course not. That's too predictable. I lower my weapon and start walking toward the apartment. I start replaying the conversation with Roger, thinking about Houston. Could this be Houston? I don't sense anything when I'm with him.

I pass another alleyway and shine my light in it. Nothing. I repeat this for blocks and decide I'm acting like a fool. I'm letting this monster control me. I'm almost home when Kane calls. "I'm pulling out of the airport on my way to the apartment now. Where are you?"

"About to be home."

"Good," he says softly. "I'll see you in half an hour, *at home*, Lilah Love." He disconnects.

I smile and stick my phone and flashlight back in my bag, but as I pass the alleyway a block from the building, a punch of awareness rushes over me. I pause, grab the flashlight, and pull my weapon. I turn and point them both, beaming the light, and holy fuck. There she is. A woman with an umbrella. I take a step forward and a red light beams on my chest from her hand. Fuck. It's not Williams. *It's him.* He's dressed like a woman, in a blonde wig, and he's here for one reason. He's here for me.

"Shoot me!" I shout. "That's the only way you get me."

Music starts playing, Phantom of the Opera, I think, which I know from my mother because I hate that shit. I take a step closer. "Go ahead," I taunt him. "Shoot me."

I just need to get close enough to confirm it really is him, not an innocent victim, and I'll shoot him, I'll kill him. This will be over. I step closer to him and damn it to fuck, Jay suddenly launches himself in front of me, and holy fuck, Umbrella Man's gun goes off. Jay crumbles to the ground. Blood gushes from his shoulder and I kneel down. "He wouldn't have shot me, you fool," I hiss, shoving my hand on his chest, trying to stop the bleeding.

"Go to him!" a familiar voice, Detective Williams' voice, calls out from somewhere in the corner. "Drop your gun and come, or he *will* kill him. He will. He will. He's crazy, Agent Love." Her voice is quaking, and I shine my flashlight to find her in the corner, her arms bound.

The light at my chest moves to Jay.

"No," Jay hisses. "No. You don't go—"

"He'll kill you, Jay. I have to go. I have to kill him first."

"No!" He grabs my arm.

"Hold the wound or you'll bleed out." I jerk my hand from his and stand up, stepping over him.

And I do what I was always destined to do. I walk toward the Umbrella Man.

THE END...FOR NOW

***

Readers,

Thank you so much for picking up LOVE ME DEAD! I know this cliffhanger was a doozy, but Lilah took me by surprise with this crazy ending that she *fucking* demanded. Sometimes, I just have to listen to my characters, but you won't need to wait long for the conclusion to this case. LOVE KILLS will be out in October and is available for pre-order everywhere now!

PRE-ORDER AND LEARN MORE HERE:
HTTPS://LILAHSERIES.WEEBLY.COM/

***

What's next for me? **DIRTY RICH SECRETS**, the next standalone book in my Dirty Rich series is out on July 30th, yes of this year, yes as in a week of this book releasing. I hope you'll check it out! This is Ashley's book, you met in her DIRTY RICH CINDERELLA STORY, if you read it, but there's no need to read any book prior to diving into DIRTY RICH SECRETS!

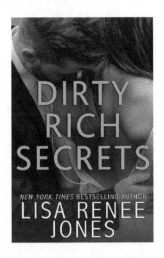

PRE-ORDER AND LEARN MORE HERE:

HTTPS://DIRTYRICH.WEEBLY.COM/DIRTY-RICH-SECRETS.HTML

***

KEEP READING FOR THE FIRST CHAPTER OF A PERFECT LIE, MY FIRST PSYCHOLOGICAL THRILLER, AND THE FIRST CHAPTER OF ONE MAN—THE FIRST BOOK IN MY NEW NAKED TRILOGY!

***

DON'T FORGET, IF YOU WANT TO BE THE FIRST TO KNOW ABOUT UPCOMING BOOKS, GIVEAWAYS, SALES AND ANY OTHER EXCITING NEWS I HAVE TO SHARE PLEASE BE SURE YOU'RE SIGNED UP FOR

MY NEWSLETTER! AS AN ADDED BONUS EVERYONE RECEIVES A FREE EBOOK WHEN THEY SIGN-UP!

HTTP://LISARENEEJONES.COM/NEWSLETTER-SIGN-UP/

A PERFECT LIE

I am Hailey Anne Monroe. I'm twenty-eight years old. An artist, who found her muse on the canvas because I wasn't allowed to have friends or even keep a journal. And yes, if you haven't guessed by now, I'm that Hailey Anne Monroe, daughter to Thomas Frank Monroe, the man who was a half-percentage point from becoming President of the United States. If you were able to ask him, he'd probably tell you that I was the half point. But you can't ask him, and he can't tell you. He's dead. They're all dead and now I can speak.

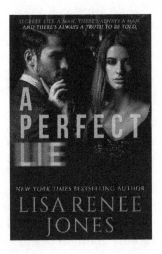

CHAPTER ONE OF A PERFECT LIE

Hailey Anne Monroe

You already know that I'm one of those perfect lies we've discussed, a façade of choices that were never my own. But that one perfect lie is too simplistic to describe who, and what, I am. I am perhaps a dozen perfect lies, the creation of at least one of those lies beginning the day I was born. That's when the clock started ticking. That's when decisions started being made for me. That's when every step that could be taken was to ensure I was "perfect." My mother, a brilliant doctor, ensured I was one hundred percent healthy, in all ways a test, pin prick, and inspection could ensure. I was, of course, vaccinated on a strict schedule, because in my household we must be so squeaky clean that we cannot possibly give anything to anyone.

Meanwhile, my father, the consummate politician, began planning my college years while my diapers were still being changed. I would be an attorney. I would go to an Ivy League college. I would be a part of the elite. Therefore, I was with tutors before I could spell. I was in dance at five years old. Of course, there was also piano, and French, Spanish, and Chinese language classes. The one joy I found was in an art class, which my mother suggested when I was twelve. It became my obsession, my one salvation, my one escape. Outside of her. She was not like my father. She was my friend, not my dictator. She was the bridge between us. The one we both adored. She listened to me. She listened to him. She tried to find compromise between us. She gave me choices, within the limits I was allowed. She tried to make me happy. She did make me as happy as anyone who was a puppet to a political machine could be, but the bigger the machine, the more developed, the harder that became. And still she fought for me.

I loved my mother with all of my heart and soul.

That's why it's hard to tell this part of my story. If there was one moment, beyond my birth, that established my destiny, and my influence on the destiny of those around me, it would be one evening during my senior year in high school, the night I killed my mother.

***

THE PAST—TWELVE YEARS AGO...

226

The steps leading to the Michaels' home seem to stretch eternally, but then so do most on this particular strip of houses in McLean, Virginia, where the rich, and sometimes famous, reside. Music radiates from the walls of the massive white mansion that is our destination, the stretch of land owned by the family wide enough that the nearest neighbor sees nothing and hears nothing. They most certainly don't know that while the Michaels are out of town, their son, Jesse, is throwing a party.

"I can't believe we're at Jesse's house," Danielle says, linking her arm through mine, something she's been doing for the past six years, since we met in private school at age eleven. Only then I was the tall one, and now I'm five-foot-four to her five-foot-eight, and that's when I'm wearing heels and she's not.

"Considering his father bloodies my father on his news program nightly, I can't either," I say. "I shouldn't be here, Danielle."

She stops walking and turns to me, her beautiful chestnut hair, which goes with her beautiful, perfect face and body, blowing right smack into my average face. She shoves said beautiful hair behind her ears, and glowers at me. "Hailey—"

"Don't start," I say, folding my arms in front of my chest, which is at least respectable, considering my dirty blonde hair and blue eyes are what I call average and others call cute. Like I'm not smart enough to know that means average. "I'm here. You already got me here."

"Jesse doesn't care about your father's run for President," she argues. "Or that his father doesn't support your father."

"Why did you just say that?" I demand.

"Say what?"

"Now you've just reminded me that I'm at the house of a man who doesn't support my father, whom I happen to love. I need to leave." I start down the stairs.

Danielle hops in front of me. "Wait. Please. I think I might be in love with Jesse. You can't just leave."

"My God, woman, you're a drama queen. You have never even kissed him. And I have to study for the SAT and so do you."

"Please. His father isn't here. His father will never know about the party or us."

"Danielle, if my father finds out—"

"He's out of town, too. How is he going to find out?"

"What about your father? He's an advisor to my father. You can't date Jesse."

She draws in a deep breath, her expression tightening before she gushes out, "*Hailey,*" making my name a plea. "I'm trying so hard to be normal. I know that you deal with things by studying. I do, but I need this. I need to feel normal."

Normal.

That word punches me with a fist of emotions I reject every time I hear it and feel them. "We will never be normal again and you know it. We weren't normal to start with. Not when—"

"After that night," she says. "We were normal enough until then. But since—after what happened, after we—"

"Stop," I hiss. "We don't talk about it. We don't talk about it *ever.*"

"Ouch," she says, grabbing my hand that is on her arm, my grip anything but gentle. "You're hurting me."

I have to count to three and force myself to breathe again before my fingers ease from her arm. "We agreed that 'the incident' was buried."

"Right," she says, and now she's hugging herself. "Because we're so good at burying things."

"We have to be," I bite out, trying to soften my tone and failing. "I *know* you know that."

She gives me several choppy nods. "Yes." Her voice is tiny. "I know." She turns pragmatic, her tone lifting. "I just need more to clutter up my mind than the SAT exam. That will come and go."

"And then there will be more work ahead."

"I need more," she insists. "I need to be normal."

"You will never—"

"I can pretend, okay? I need to *feel* normal even if I'm not. And even if you don't admit it, so do you."

My fingers curl, my nails cutting into my palms, perhaps because she's right. Some part of me cared when I put on my best black jeans and a V-neck black sweater that shows my assets. Some part of me wanted to look as good as she does in her pink lacy off-the-shoulder blouse and faded jeans. Some part of me forgot that the "normal" ship sailed for me the day I was born to a father who aspired to be President, but still, I don't disagree with her. I need to get her head on straight and maybe kissing Jesse is exactly the distraction that she needs do the trick. I link my arm with hers once more. "Let's go see Jesse."

She gives me one of her big smiles and I know that I've made the right decision, because when she's smiling like that no one sees anything but beauty which is exactly how it needs to stay. And so, I make that walk with her up those steps, climbing toward what I hope is not a bad decision, when I swore I was done with those. Nevertheless, in a matter of two minutes, we're on the giant concrete porch, a Selena Gomez song radiating from the walls and rattling my teeth.

The door flies open, and several kids I've seen around, but don't know, stagger outside while Danielle pulls me into the gaudy glamour of the Michaels' home, which is as far opposite of my conservative father as the talk show host's politics. The floors are white and gray marble. The furniture is boxy and flat, with red and orange accents, with the added flair of newly added bottles, bags, cups, and people. There are lots of people everywhere, including on top of the grand piano. It's like my high school class, inclusive of the football team and cheerleaders, has been dropped inside a bad Vegas hotel room. Or so I've heard and seen in movies. I've not actually been to Vegas; that would be far too scandalous for a future first daughter, or so says my father.

"Where now?" I ask, leaning into Danielle.

"He said the backyard," she replies, scanning. "This way!" she adds, and suddenly she's dragging me through several groups of about a half-dozen bodies.

Our destination is apparently the outdoor patio, where a fire is burning in a stone pit, and despite it being April, and in the sixties, surrounded by a cluster of ottoman-like seating and lanterns on steel poles. Plus, more people are here, and now instead of Selena Gomez rattling my teeth, it's Rihanna.

"Danielle!" The shout comes from Jesse, who is sitting in a cluster of people to our far left. Of course, Danielle starts dragging me forward again, which has me feeling like her cute dog that doesn't want to be walked. Correction: Her forgotten dog that doesn't want to be walked, considering she lets go of me and runs to Jesse, giving him a big hug. I'm left with one open seat, smack between two football players: David Nelson and Ramon Miller. Both are hot. Both have dark hair, though Ramon's is curly and excessive, and David's is buzzed, understandably since I think I heard his dad is military. Okay, I know his dad is military because I've been crushing on him since he showed up at school six months ago.

I sit awkwardly between them, and stare desperately at Danielle, who just stuck her tongue down Jesse's throat in a familiar way that says it's not the first time. *I need to leave*, I think. I'll just get up and leave, but then, what if she panics? What if she forgets that Jesse can't be in on 'the incident'? We can never tell anyone what happened. Why did I think this night was a good distraction?

"Hey there," David says, piercing me with his blue eyes.

"Hi," I say.

"You look like you want to crawl under a rock," he comments.

"Do you know where I can find one?"

He laughs. He has a good laugh. A genuine laugh and since I don't know many people who do anything genuinely, I feel that hard spot in my belly begin to soften. "I'll help you find one if you take me with you."

"You don't belong under a rock," I say.

He arches a brow. "And you do?"

"Belong," I say. "No. But happier there right now, yes."

"That hurts my feelings," he says, holding his hand to his chest as if wounded.

"Oh. No. Sorry. I just meant...I don't do parties."

"Because your dad is a politician," he assumes.

"He doesn't exactly approve of events like this."

He laughs again. "Events. Right." His hand settles on my leg and there is this funny sensation in my belly. "I'll make sure nothing goes wrong. Okay?"

"No. No, I'll make sure nothing goes wrong."

He leans in and presses his cheek to mine, his lips by my ear. "Then I'll give you extra protection." I inhale, and he pulls back, suddenly no longer touching me.

My gaze lifts and I find Danielle looking at me with a big grin on her face. David hands me a shot glass and Jesse hands Danielle one. She nods, and I don't know why, but I just do it. I down the liquid in what is my first drink ever. The next thing I know, David's tongue is down my throat and when I blink, I'm not even sitting on the back patio anymore. I'm lying on a bed and he's pulling his shirt off. And I don't know how I got here. I don't know what is happening. Panic rises with a sense of being out of control. I stand up and David reaches for me, but I shove at him.

"No!"

I dart around him and I must be drunk but I think my feet are too steady to be drunk. I run from the room and keep running down a hallway and to the stairs. I grab the railing, flashes of images in my mind. David offering me another drink. Me refusing. David kissing me and offering me yet another drink. I had refused. So why was I just on a bed and unaware of how I got there?

"Hailey!"

At the sound of David's voice, I take off down the steps, not even sure where I'm going, but I don't stop. I push through bodies and I'm on the porch in what feels like slow motion. I'm running down the stairs. I'm leaving. I have to get out of here.

***

I blink awake, cold, with a hard surface at my back. Gasping with the shock of disorientation, I sit up, the first orange and red of a new day in the darkness of the sky. I'm outside. I'm...I look around and realize that I'm on the bench of a picnic table. I'm in a park. I stand up and start to pace. I'm dressed in black jeans and a black sweater. The party. I went to the party. I dig my heels in. Did I get drunk? Wouldn't I feel sick? I'm not sick. I'm not unsteady. My tiny purse I carry with me often is at my hip. I unzip it and pull out my phone. Ten calls from my mother. No messages from Danielle.

"Danielle," I whisper. "Where is Danielle?"

I dial her number and she doesn't answer. I dial again. And again. I press my hand to my face and look at the time. Five in the morning. My car is at Jesse's house. I start walking, looking for a sign, anything to tell me where I'm at. Finally, I find a sign: *Rock Creek Park*. The party was in McLean. Rock Creek is back in Washington, a good forty minutes away. I lean against the sign and my mother calls again.

I answer. "Mom?"

"Thank God," she breathes out, her voice filled with both panic and anger, two things that my mother, a gentle soul, and doctor, who loves people, rarely allows to surface. "Oh, thank God. I've been so worried."

"I don't know what happened, Mom. I blacked out and I'm at a park."

"Near Rock Creek," she says. "I know. I did the 'find my phone' search but it's not exact and I was about to call the police. I just knew—" She sobs before adding, "I just knew you were dead in the woods. I was about to get help. I was about to have a search start."

"I—Mom, I—"

"Go to the main parking lot." She hangs up.

My cellphone rings with Danielle's number. "Where are you?" I demand.

"At Jesse's," she says. "Where are you? I was asleep and I thought you were in a room with David, but he was with some other girl."

"You don't know what happened to me?" I ask.

"No. Jesus. What happened?"

Headlights shine in my direction from a parking lot. "I'll call you later," I say. "I have to deal with my mother." I hang up and start running toward the lights. By the time I'm at the driver's side of my mother's Mercedes, she's there, too, out of the car and reaching for me.

"You have so much to explain," she attacks, grabbing my arms and hugging me. "I am furious with you. You scared me."

"I scared me, too," I say hugging her, starting to cry, the scent of her jasmine perfume, consuming my senses, and calming me. "I don't know what happened."

She pulls back. "Did you drink and do drugs?"

"No. I mean—one drink. I'm fine. I—"

"One drink. We both know what that means. This wasn't the first time."

"No. Mom. It was. One drink. I don't know what happened. Someone drugged me. They had to have drugged me."

Her lips purse. "Get in the car."

"Mom—"

"Get in the car."

I nod and do as I'm told. I get in the car. The minute she's in with me, I try to explain. "Mom, I—"

"Do not speak to me until I calm down." He seatbelt warning beeps.

"Mom—"

"Shut up, Hailey," she says, putting us in motion.

I suck in air at the harsh words that do not fit my mother, who is not just beautiful, but graceful in her actions and words. Perfect, actually, and everything I aspire to be. I click my belt while her warning continues to go off. She turns us onto the highway and I listen to the warning going off, trying to fill the blank space in my head with answers I can give her. But there are none and suddenly she lets out a choked sound and hits the brakes. My eyes jolt open, but everything is spinning. We're spinning. I can't see or move. "Mom!" I shout, I think. Or maybe I don't. Glass shatters. I feel it on my face, cutting me, digging into my skin.

We jolt again, no longer spinning, but the world goes black.

Time is still.

And then there are sirens and I try to catch my breath, but my chest hurts so badly. "Mom," I whisper, turning to look at her but she's not there. She's not there. Panic rises fast and hard and I unhook my belt and ball my fist at my aching chest. Forcing myself to move, I sit up to find my mother on the hood of the car, a huge chunk of steel through her body.

I scream and I can't stop screaming. I can't stop screaming.

ORDER A PERFECT LIE HERE:
HTTPS://APERFECTLIEBOOK.WEEBLY.COM

THE NAKED TRILOGY

BOOK ONE IS AVAILABLE EVERYWHERE NOW! BOOKS TWO AND THREE ARE AVAILABLE FOR PRE-ORDER!

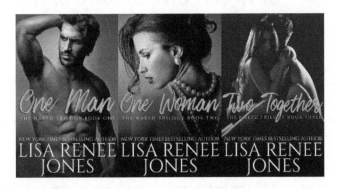

One man can change everything. That man can touch you and you tremble all over. That man can wake you up and allow you to breathe when life leaves you unable to catch your breath. For me that ONE MAN is Jax North. He's handsome, brutally so, and wealthy, money and power easily at his fingertips. He's dark, and yet, he can make me smile with a single look or word. He's a force when he walks into a room.

Our first encounter is intense, overwhelmingly intense. I go with it. I go with him and how can I not? He's that ONE MAN for me and what a ride it is. But there are things about me that he doesn't know, he can't know, so I say goodbye. Only you don't say goodbye to a man like Jax if he doesn't want you to. I've challenged him without trying. He wants me. I don't want to want him, and yet, I crave him. He tears me down, my resistance, my walls. But those walls protect me. They seal my secrets inside. And I forget that being alone is safe. I forget that there are reasons I can't be with

Jax North. I forget that once he knows, everything will change.

Because I need him. Because he's my ONE MAN.

CHAPTER ONE OF ONE MAN

Jax...

The moon glows with white light and hangs low and round over the nearby ocean darkened by night as if it, like the hundreds of guests in the garden of one of the San Francisco Knight hotels, is watching the beautiful brunette and star of the night. Emma Knight, the twenty-eight-year-old heiress to the hotel chain's worldwide empire, and who, in fact, lost her father one month ago. Now, her brother Chance rules their hotel empire and her mother has fled to Europe for reasons few, I suspect Emma included, knows.

But I know.

She stands next to Randall Montgomery, her brother's right-hand and confidant, a man who might be fit enough and decent enough looking if he didn't act like he has a stick up his ass. A man on my radar for reasons he'll soon regret. He wants Emma and her money. She is the furthest down the food chain of them all, and based on her history with her father, even further down than would be expected. No doubt, she inherited with her father's death, but I wouldn't be shocked to discover she was given a token instead of a goldmine.

The announcer stands at a podium and begins lavishly speaking of Emma's father with purpose. Tonight, with women in fancy gowns and men in tuxedos, ice carved into sculptures and champagne poured in glasses, Emma is here to accept a philanthropy award on his behalf while her brother is curiously absent. If he were here, I wouldn't be here. Neither I nor any of the North family could stand her father, not that I find her brother any more palatable. Her father is gone, though, and now Emma is the proverbial queen of the hour. And the queen, unaware that she is, has had my attention for quite some time.

There's irony in the fact that I, Jax North, the eldest now of the living North family offspring is, in fact, the man who watches her. An irony she'll understand soon, but not too soon. For now, I stand at one of the rows of white-clothed tables, deep enough beyond in the crowd of people to be as good as in the shadows, a man whose family has done business with her family for decades, though l have been in the shadows in those endeavors just as I am here now. Present but unseen.

Emma steps to the podium, but not before I catch a glimpse of her pale pink floor-length dress that is elegant in its simplicity, in the way it highlights her slender but womanly figure. Her hands grip the sides of the podium and for a long moment, a full minute at least, she simply looks out across the crowd but doesn't speak. There's a charge of expectation in the room, a sense of the crowd pushing her to speak and when finally, her pink-painted lips part, the microphone crackles and squeaks. This seems to jolt her and she laughs nervously, a soft sweet laugh to match her sweet little ass. Perhaps the only sweet things about the Knight family.

"Thank you all for being here," she finally says, and her voice is strained but suitably strong. "It's emotional to be here tonight, among those honored who are living while my father is no longer with us. To be here at a hotel that was the center of the world for him." She cuts her stare and I can almost feel her struggling for composure, the way I struggle when I speak of my older brother.

"I loved my father so very much," Emma adds, and the pain in her voice is it for me. I run a hand over the silk of my light blue tie, barely contained impatience in the action, but tonight isn't the time; it's not when I'm meant to find Emma and Emma me. It's a thought that has me turning away and disappearing into the gardens, entering the hotel by a side door. I'm here in this hotel for one reason: Emma. She's here and it's long past due that we meet. It's long past due that she learns about the connection between her family and mine. I stroll a carpeted hallway with elegant chandeliers dipping low at strategic locations, about to turn into the bar when I come face to face with Eric Mitchell, a man who is quite literally a genius. He's also vice president in one of the largest corporations in the world.

"Long time, man," he greets, offering me his hand. It's a strong hand, and when I look into his blue eyes, I see the man born a savant, the man who see numbers more than words. I see the man who helped Bennett Enterprises reach beyond a legal powerhouse to a conglomerate, even before acquiring an NFL team.

"Doesn't Bennett own hotels, which would make you the Knights' competition?"

His lips curve. "Keep your friends close and your enemies closer. I went to school with Chance. Good guy."

Good guy my fucking ass. "We should talk."

"About?"

"All things green. How about lunch tomorrow?"

"I can make that happen. "

We set-up the meeting and the ways this little encounter has inspired me are many. I cut right into a dimly lit bar that's desolate at the moment and thank fuck for it. The damn hotel is filled to the rim for that awards ceremony. Alone suits me just fine right about now and I walk to the back of the bar and sit down in a red leather booth that overlooks a room with couches, cushy chairs, and dangling lights but also provides a curtain for privacy. The Knight name is all about luxury and comfort, but at its core, it's about greed. At my core right now, I'm about that speech Emma was giving, about the pain at its core. That pain is why I'm here.

A waiter appears and I order whiskey, North Whiskey, my family's whiskey, which is in every Knight hotel in the country and beyond. I don't give a fuck if it stays or goes or I wouldn't be here. "Bring the bottle."

He's just filled my glass, and the glass is at my lips when Emma walks into the bar. Alone. She's done her time on stage and ran for cover. The hotel might be hosting the event, but she isn't. She's halfway into the bar when voices sound behind her. She peeks over her shoulder and then with a panicked look, darts in my direction.

To my surprise—and I don't surprise easily—she slides into the booth with me and pulls the curtain shut. "So sorry," she says, claiming the seat next to me. "I really need to avoid a conversation and well, breathe a moment or ten. The only way to do that is to be having a private meeting that looks as if it's just that: private, not to be disturbed." She takes my glass and downs my whiskey.

Interesting that she didn't run to Randall for comfort, but in fact ran away from him.

She glances at me, and when her beautiful pale green eyes flecked with amber meet mine, there is a charge between us, an awareness that parts her lips and has her turning away from me. Because she knows who I am?

"I'll buy that bottle of whiskey for you," she says, "for letting me intrude."

A statement that either proves she has no idea who I am or that she's playing me the way a Knight will play.

It doesn't really matter. It's like the sky opened up and delivered her right to me. "Considering I'm a North and that's North Whiskey," I say, refilling the glass. "I think I can handle paying for the bottle and helping the lady of the night hide out."

Her eyes go wide. "You're Jax North." She blinks. "Of course you are. You look like the North family, all tall, blond, and handsomely brooding." She drinks a bit more. "And that's the whiskey making me overly verbal. My father didn't approve of me being overly verbal."

Except she just downed that whiskey and hasn't been drinking all night. She's nervous, rambling in a rather charming, vulnerable way that I find attractive, for reasons I don't try to understand.

"I didn't know 'overly verbal' was a thing."

"You didn't know my father well, then. Actually, no one did." She swallows hard. "Back to you." It's a hard push from any question I might have made about that statement "no one did." "You really do look like your father and brother. I can't believe I didn't immediately place you."

"You mean Hunter, I assume, since my younger brother, Brody, beats to his own drum. A drum that doesn't include running the core whiskey operation or any involvement with the Knight Hotel brand."

"Yes, Hunter," she says, and there's a flicker in her eyes, an understanding that we're talking about a brother that is no more with us on this earth than her father. "I met them both, briefly. I ah—"

I narrow my eyes on her waiting for her to finish that sentence, prodding when she does not. "You what?"

"You—"

"Lost them both, as you did your father," I supply. "Yes. My father to a ski accident, a year ago next week. Six months ago next month for my brother." I leave out the cause of death. That isn't a place either of us wants me to go with the Knight family tonight. "And yes," I add, "time helps, but anyone who tells you it makes the cut heal is lying. It just stops the bleeding."

"Thank you for saying that," she says in a deep breath, "because if one more person tells me time will make it better, I might scream." She softens her voice. "I'm sad to say that I barely knew your father and brother, and only know you now because of this moment in time, that you neither chose nor invited."

"Should I have?"

"Why would you? You don't know me." She laughs a bitter laugh. "Well, there is my family money. That's what everyone knows and wants. They think they know my worth, but they know nothing."

I don't ask what that means. I dare to slide closer to her. I dare to allow my leg to press to hers, the current between us charming the air. "I am a North, which means that I have power and money. I don't need yours."

"Money feeds greed. What you have is never enough."

"There are other things to want besides money."

"Do you know who I am?"

"Emma Knight."

"Can I deny that perhaps for the rest of my life?"

I lean closer, the scent of her distinctly warm—amber and vanilla, I believe—my interest in this woman piqued in both expected and unexpected ways. "Why would you want to?"

"A complicated answer to a simple question." Her voice cracks and she turns away from me. She reaches for my glass again and downs every drop in it. She sets it down.

"More?" I ask.

She glances over at me. "Yes, but I should warn you that I'm a very bad drinker."

I refill the glass and sip before handing it to her. She stares at the glass before her gaze lifts to my mouth. Unlike moments before, she's now thinking of exactly what I intended: about her mouth where my mouth was moments before. "I promise to catch you if you fall," I say softly.

"Don't start this relationship off by making promises you won't even try to keep."

Relationship. She's planning on this encounter leading to more, which of course could simply be because I'm now in charge of my family empire, not just the contact for all things both North and Knight. Or perhaps it's more. I plan to make it more.

"I never make a promise I don't keep," I say, and I will catch her if she falls, because once I catch her, she's mine. Once she's mine, everything comes full circle.

"Never?"

"Never," I assure her, "which is something my friends value and my enemies dread."

"Do you have many enemies?"

"A man or woman with money and power always has enemies."

Her cellphone rings and she pants out a breath. "Of course. They're now looking for me by calling me." She pulls her cell from her purse and glances at the number.

"Randall?" I ask.

Her gaze jerks to mine. "How do you know that and him?"

"I know a lot of people. Enemies everywhere, Emma," I say softly, and I find myself really wanting her to listen. Really wanting to protect her, which is a contradiction to everything I would do otherwise where the Knights are concerned. "And this one wants to be in your bed. If he isn't already."

"How do you know that?"

"I told you. I know a lot of people and things."

She sets her phone on the table without answering him. "You aren't going to answer?"

"No. I'm not going to answer. I'm not ready to go back."

"Would like to get out of here?"

"And go where?"

"A castle by the ocean."

She laughs. "If only."

"I'm serious, Emma. Come with me. I'll take you away."

"Would you be asking me that if I walked away from it all?"

The curtain pulls back and Randall is standing there, his dark hair slicked back, his gaze sliding between the two of us and landing on me. "What the fuck are you doing here, Jax?"

My lips quirk. "Enjoying good company and good whiskey." I glance at Emma. "With a beautiful woman," I add.

I expect her to blush and look away, but she doesn't. For several beats she just looks at me, her stare unreadable, but the crackle in the air between us, the whip and pull of attraction, is damn near palpable.

"Emma," Randall snaps, "you have people here honoring your father."

"Right. Responsibility calls." Her eyes, her sea-green eyes meet mine. "Thank you, Jax. For the company and the fine whiskey." Randall offers her his hand, but she ignores it and stands up.

"Don't you want the answer to your question?" I ask.

She glances behind her, over her shoulder, to meet my stare. "Yes, I do." But she doesn't stay for an answer. She walks away, doing the impossible, considering she's a Knight and I'm a North, as she does. She makes me crave more of her, but that changes nothing. I came here, seeking her out, for a reason. That reason hasn't changed.

LEARN MORE AND BUY HERE:
HTTPS://NAKEDTRILOGY.WEEBLY.COM/

ALSO BY LISA RENEE JONES

THE INSIDE OUT SERIES

If I Were You
Being Me
Revealing Us
*His Secrets**
Rebecca's Lost Journals
*The Master Undone**
*My Hunger**
No In Between
*My Control**
I Belong to You
*All of Me**

THE SECRET LIFE OF AMY BENSEN

Escaping Reality
Infinite Possibilities
Forsaken
*Unbroken**

CARELESS WHISPERS

Denial
Demand
Surrender

WHITE LIES

Provocative
Shameless

TALL, DARK & DEADLY

Hot Secrets

244

Dangerous Secrets
Beneath the Secrets

WALKER SECURITY

Deep Under
Pulled Under
Falling Under

LILAH LOVE

Murder Notes
Murder Girl
Love Me Dead
Love Kills (October 2019)

DIRTY RICH

Dirty Rich One Night Stand
Dirty Rich Cinderella Story
Dirty Rich Obsession
Dirty Rich Betrayal
Dirty Rich Cinderella Story: Ever After
Dirty Rich One Night Stand: Two Years Later
Dirty Rich Obsession: All Mine
Dirty Rich Secrets

THE FILTHY TRILOGY

The Bastard
The Princess
The Empire

THE NAKED TRILOGY

One Man
One Woman (September 2019)
Two Together (November 2019)

ABOUT THE AUTHOR

New York Times and USA Today bestselling author Lisa Renee Jones is the author of the highly acclaimed INSIDE OUT series.

In addition to the success of Lisa's INSIDE OUT series, she has published many successful titles. The TALL, DARK AND DEADLY series and THE SECRET LIFE OF AMY BENSEN series, both spent several months on a combination of the *New York Times* and USA Today bestselling lists. Lisa is also the author of the bestselling LILAH LOVE and WHITE LIES series.

Prior to publishing, Lisa owned multi-state staffing agency that was recognized many times by The Austin Business Journal and also praised by the Dallas Women's Magazine. In 1998 Lisa was listed as the #7 growing women owned business in Entrepreneur Magazine.

Lisa loves to hear from her readers. You can reach her on Twitter and Facebook daily.